CLAUS AND EFFECT

THE TINK HOLLY CHRONICLES
BOOK 2

ABIGAIL DRAKE

ONE

I hated pole dancing. I hated dancing in general, but for a Christmas elf like me, pole dancing presented a unique set of challenges. Frostbite was definitely a concern. As was the unfortunate combination of moist, exposed flesh and a frozen candy cane striped pole.

Ouch.

I once heard about a dancer who had to be surgically removed from a pole when her private parts got stuck. Agonizing, yet it worked out well for her in the end. Yes, she lost part of her hoo-haw, but she married one of the firefighters who rescued her and now has two little elflings of her own and a home in the suburbs.

Not that I wanted to follow in her stripper-heeled footsteps. At this point, I had no desire for elflings and preferred to keep all my private parts intact, but I was working undercover on a drug case we'd been trying to crack at the EBI— the Elven Bureau of Investigation. As a special civilian consultant in the Christmas Crimes Division, this case could make or break me.

"Tinklebelle Holly, are you ready yet? You'll be on in a few minutes."

Scarlet Knickers, a former exotic dancer and the new owner of the Sugarbums Dancing in Your Head Strip Club (known to locals as Sugarbums), stood nervously in the dressing room entrance, waiting for me. She planned to change the place's name to Ms. Scarlet's but hadn't gotten the signage yet.

I gave her a nod. "Ready as I'll ever be."

Scarlet and I went way back. She'd once filed a restraining order against me, but it had been a total misunderstanding. I'd gotten wasted one night and bumped into her as she performed, knocking her into a snowbank—a complete accident and, in my mind, an occupational hazard for a stripper working on the North Pole. She'd disagreed, but she'd forgiven me for it long ago.

Or at least I hoped she had.

But I knew she stood firmly on our side regarding the investigation. Her daughter, Ruby, had died of a candicocane overdose a few months ago. Scarlet felt convinced that there was a lot more to it than a simple overdose. It may have been nothing but a grieving mother's pain, but I thought she might be right. There were too many things that didn't add up.

My super-hot and sexy boss, the dark elf Jax Grayson, and I had stopped the elves responsible for distributing the highly addictive drug all over the elven world, but a new cartel had stepped in. Now a more potent and deadly form of the drug had hit the streets, and Ruby was just one of many innocent elves who had fallen victim to it.

They called it "rock candy," since this particular form of candicocane hit the user hard—like a rock to the head. Also, it resembled old-fashioned rock candy rather than the original version of the drug, which had been in powdered form. Some clever elf had figured out that adding water to the powdered drug and boiling it down increased potency. Kind of like a chef doing a reduction sauce. Except, this reduction wasn't rich and yummy. This had very deadly consequences.

Scarlet had given me a tip that her daughter's ex, Algae Winkle, would be coming to the club for the Halloween party tonight with information we could use. Since we'd had no leads and there were several warrants out for Al's arrest on other crimes, Scarlet's info could be just the ticket we needed to crack the case.

Unfortunately, I knew Jax wouldn't see it that way, so I'd cleverly avoided telling him I planned to be here this evening. I'd also avoided telling my partner, Nativity Bing, that this wasn't exactly an official operation. Bing thought we had permission to be here. I lied, but I had no other choice. I'd gotten the tip this morning. Time was of the essence. If I'd done things by the book, it would have taken days to set this up, and Al Winkle would be long gone.

Scarlet and I had a plan. A simple one. She'd approach Al first and get the info she wanted about Ruby's death. I'd arrest him afterwards on an outstanding warrant.

Easy peasy.

We'd both be happy. I'd get a crook, and hopefully Scarlet would get the answers she so desperately needed.

"Ruby was only twenty-six years old. She had terrible taste in men, but she'd never been a druggie. There is something else going on here. And there is someone else involved. There is something else going on here. And there is someone else involved."

"What will you do when you find out who it is?" I asked, adjusting my red push-up bra. My boobs had never looked so big. I couldn't stop staring at them. That may have been the point.

"I'm not going to hurt them if that's what you're thinking." Scarlet let out a weary sigh. "But I will do whatever I can to make them stop hurting other people. That's all I want. It's not about revenge. I'm angry about Ruby's death, but the thirst for revenge rots you from the inside out. That's why I want to use my anger productively. When something like this happens, you have two choices: bitter or better. I choose to make things better, not to let myself become bitter. Does that make sense?"

"It does. You're a good person, Scarlet."

Her red lips quirked in a smile. "I know. And you're a good person, too. You saved a lot of lives last year. Maybe you can do that again this year."

Last Christmas, Jax and I had figured out who distributed the powdered form of this dangerous drug all over the elven world. The culprits had been friends of mine, Sugar Happypie and her nephew Frank Yummy, but the plot had also involved several of Santa's reindeer. Sugar, Frank, and Comet (the worst reindeer of them all) had died in a freak fire in the stables. Jax and I nearly died as well. I got lots of attention both for helping solve the case and because Santa (the big guy himself) was my uncle. The Holly family name had always been a lot to live up to, and until I found my calling at the EBI, I'd been a hot mess, but I'd changed that through pure force of will.

The only problem? Many elves thought my success in solving that case had been a fluke. Sometimes, even I thought it may have been a fluke, but Scarlet did not, which was why I stood in her club in a thong about to pole dance. I wanted to help her, but I also had to figure this out and prove to everyone, including myself, that I could do this.

The body count had risen steadily over the last few months, and things seemed to worsen by the day. We had to solve this and do it quickly before more innocent elves paid the price.

Sadly, the case had stumped us, and we had not made progress for weeks.

We knew the drugs came from the rainforests of the nature elf community, but we didn't know the elves behind it or how the drugs entered the North Pole. Al, a nature elf, had been friends with the late Frank Yummy. It seemed like the perfect lead, and I'd jumped at the chance. And now I was about to parade around nearly naked in front of a room full of spectators.

"Are you sure I look okay?" I asked. I wore a small, red, satin mask to disguise my identity. The mask may have been the largest thing I had on at the moment, but if someone looked closely enough, they might recognize me.

Hopefully, no one would look closely enough.

Another dancer walked past me. She'd just exited the stage and had a big wad of cash in her hands. More elf bucks stuck out of her cleavage and the sides of her tiny G-string. She had the image of a rose tattooed on her bottom. I didn't see her face since she also wore a mask, but she had long, dark hair and her body was perfection. She also moved like a dancer, all graceful and elegant. She had excellent posture as well.

I straightened my shoulders. I had horrible posture. But several of Scarlet's dancers had day jobs as models and actresses. One of them told me dancing here was a great way to earn extra cash and they found it empowering. I didn't feel empowered at all.

I knew I might be making a big mistake, and not only because I was the ugly duckling of the strip club. I felt a stab of guilt at not telling Jax about this and not being honest with Bing. I tugged on my red push-up bra in a failed attempt to make it cover more of my cleavage. Somehow, I'd gone back to being a hot mess again. I hated this feeling.

Scarlet swiped my hands away. "Stop fussing. You look great, but you need more sparkle." She called over the prop guy. "Gus Gravy, we need more sparkle."

Gus, an oddly shaped elf with a limp, turned and stared at us for a long moment. At least, I thought he stared at us. He wore a full mask so I couldn't see his face. And the hood of his long cloak covered his head.

"Gus? Are you sleeping standing up again? You need to stop doing that. It's creepy. Also, Tink needs sparkle. Stat. Come on, buddy."

He seemed to come out of whatever trance he'd been under and handed Scarlet a can of spray-on glitter. As soon as she took it, he shuffled away without saying a word.

"Is he alright?" I asked, watching him.

"He's fine. He marches a step or two behind the parade if you know what I mean. He loves Halloween, though. He gets into it. I guess he's Quasimodo this year, but his hump is in the wrong place. It's dead center on his back." She pointed the can of glitter at my face, only an inch away from my nose. "Time to shine. Close your eyes, or you'll be blind."

I shut them just in time.

"Watch it with that stuff," I said as she covered my face, hair, and body in glitter. "Don't go crazy."

"There is no such thing as too much glitter." She gave me one final squirt. "Done. You look fabulous."

I opened my eyes. Every inch of me sparkled like a disco ball.

"Fabulous? Is that what you call this?"

"The sparkle makes the stripper. That's what I always say."

"Oh. Me, too," I said drily. She missed the sarcasm.

"I would have gone for pasties, though. I have some to match your thong, and you have the boobs to pull it off."

"Thanks," I said, inspecting my chest again.

"I mean it. You're the whole package. Great boobs. Great butt. Even that wig is amazing." She patted the bright red wig in place. It matched my bra and thong and mask perfectly. "You'll knock them dead. Also, it's a Saturday night. The entire audience is full of coal mining elves who are already blackout drunk. You could go out and polka, and they wouldn't notice the difference."

Scarlet, although at least two decades older than my own thirty years, didn't look her age. She was gorgeous and intelligent and a nice person, too. She volunteered at a cat shelter on her days off and cared for her elderly mother (a former stripper, Florina Dazzlethighs—Flo Dazzle for short). And other than that restraining order, she'd been nothing but good to me. She'd even helped me prepare for this undercover job by teaching me some moves on the stripper pole earlier today. I owed her a lot.

She put on a small mask made of red lace and tied it behind her head. It suited her, not disguising her features, or impairing her vision, but somehow festive and sexy. I'd never been good at being sexy for Halloween. I usually dressed as something funny or something stupid. I excelled at stupid.

"I didn't realize that doing the polka was an option," I said.

Scarlet rolled her eyes. "It's not. Don't be nervous. You're a natural. If I didn't know any better, I'd think you'd been stripping your whole life."

"I give off that vibe."

"You do, and it's a good one." She put her hand on my shoulders and stared deeply into my eyes. "Girls like you and me...well, we don't always get a fair shake. We're too much for some people and not enough for others, but that's okay. The only person you have to worry about is the one inside here." She poked my boob.

I blinked up at her. "Inside my boob?"

"No. In your heart." She shook her head. "Tink, you are wicked smart, but sometimes I think you have a brain full of sprinkles and marshmallows." As I tried to figure out the meaning behind her cryptic and somehow delicious-sounding words, a gong sounded. "Oh, boy. That's you. Break a leg, kiddo. Listen for your stage name."

"But I don't have a stage name."

"Oh, yes. You do." With a wink, she nudged me forward as the announcer's voice came over the loudspeaker.

"And now a special Halloween treat. A brand new dancer. This is her first time here, ladies and gentlemen. Let's have a big hand for our newest Sugarbum...Mistle Ho."

I looked over my shoulder at Scarlet. "My stage name is Mistle Ho?"

She laughed. "Payback for when you knocked me on my butt. Have fun."

I walked onstage and stumbled when the strains of "I Saw Mommy Kissing Santa Claus" came over the loudspeaker, another surprise from Scarlet. She found it amusing since my late father had been the previous Santa, and my uncle was the current one.

"Seriously?" I asked, mouthing the word to her. She laughed.

Scarlet could be a sick puppy sometimes.

The club seemed pretty full, but, as Scarlet said, most of the patrons were already drunk. About half of them got into the Halloween theme and dressed up. Half had come straight from work and didn't bother. Almost all were male.

After a quick swing around the pole, I spied my partner, Nativity Bing's, tall, handsome form in the crowd. He'd come dressed as a vampire but didn't wear a mask since he worried it could interfere with his vision. He took this seriously because he was a good cop and a good person, and I knew him well.

He'd been Officer Bing when I first met him, but we'd been promoted around the same time. He went from being a beat cop to being a detective. I'd gone from cleaning out reindeer stalls to dancing half-naked on a frozen pole in front of a bunch of drunken miners. We were both moving up in the world.

"Al Winkle is here," he said, his voice coming through the communication device in my ear. "He's by the bar."

Al's eyes darted back and forth as he waited for his drink. His narrow face seemed too small for his nose and ears. His dark hair never looked clean, but tonight he appeared even more disheveled, and his broken capillaries and rotten teeth were a testament to years of drug and alcohol abuse. Although my age, Al looked much older. He even looked older than Scarlet, but Scarlet was in great shape and took care of herself. He'd had a rough life and made bad choices, which showed. But Al could be the answer to solving our case. I felt it down to my toes.

Bing didn't seem convinced Al could provide helpful information, but he'd given me some slack. I had a feeling the slack had more to do with the fact that he currently dated my roommate and best friend, Noelle Toffee, than it had to do with my excellent detective skills, but I'd take it either way.

As I swung around the pole again, my eyes on Al, a drunken elf in the standard brown coal mining uniform, squinted up at me from the front row. "Wait, aren't you Tinklebelle Holly?"

He had to shout to be heard over the music as he studied my face. None of the miners wore costumes. They must have recently finished their shift. A stocky elf next to him with a shock of red hair burst out laughing.

"Come on, Pooky. As if Santa's niece would be dancing half-naked in this dump."

Scarlet, who'd come to scan the crowd for Al, smacked the one who'd spoken on the head. "Call my place a dump one more time, Carrots McFee, and you're out of here."

Carrots ducked his head. "Yes, ma'am."

Scarlet's eyes met mine. If my cover got blown, she could be in danger, too. "Time to dance, girly. I'm not paying you to stand there."

I grabbed the pole, spinning around it again and somehow managing not to trip in my bright red stripper heels. A voice came over the device in my ear. It was Bing.

"Uh-oh. We have a problem. Ganja Green is here too. He's at a table dead center. I didn't see him come in."

Ganja, a nature elf and a well-known crime boss, could be an unexpected complication. Most nature elves in the criminal community had some connection to Ganja, and usually they owed him either money or favors. It seemed likely that Al owed him something as well.

"Al is sweating buckets," I said into the communication device on my wrist as I shimmied around the pole. "He's going to bail."

Scarlet must have felt it too. Rather than wait for Al to

sit, as we'd planned, she walked over and began speaking with him, her back turned to me. She carried a fat, white envelope with her. She planned to pay him for information and Al eyed the envelope greedily. He seemed receptive to the idea, but as Scarlet talked, Al got twitchy. His gaze traveled nervously around the bar.

I kept my attention locked on his face. I was on high alert, watching for any change in expression or sudden movements. He mopped his forehead with a dirty handkerchief he'd pulled out of his pocket and shot another worried glance around the room. When his gaze landed on the stage, where I attempted to match my hip thrusts to the song's beat, his face went pale. He acted even more jumpy and nervous than usual, which was saying a lot. I wondered if he might be high. When his eyes locked on Ganja, fear washed over his features—not that I blamed him. Ganja was a scary guy.

Unlike most nature elves, who were laid-back and chill, Ganja loomed over the other patrons, big and intimidating. He had an aura of power and a long scar on his face that made his lip look permanently twisted into a scowl. Despite that, he was strikingly handsome. With skin like caramel, eyes the same shade as coffee, and dark hair the color of chocolate, he looked like a yummy mochaccino in sexy, mob boss form.

Although I was not usually a fan of mob bosses, I did love mochaccinos—with extra cream and a cherry on top. Ganja needed no additional toppings. He was naturally perfect and surprisingly hot.

I don't know why his attractiveness surprised me, but it did. I'd always had a thing for bad boys. Ganja was no boy, however, nor did he fall into the same category as the leather-wearing hooligans I'd gone out with occasionally to annoy my grandmother. Ganja had been involved in some unsavory stuff—prostitution, illegal gambling, Christmas cake theft—and probably candicocane trafficking. I didn't have proof of that, but it seemed likely. And Ganja showing up here tonight didn't feel like a coincidence.

Ganja's dark eyes scanned my body in a way so powerful it felt almost like a caress. It also made me feel naked. I was already pretty naked, but it made me feel more naked and oddly exposed.

I stopped twirling and thrusting and stared right back at him. I couldn't help myself. He was hypnotic.

"Tink." Bing's voice in my ear came through as an urgent hiss. "What are you doing?"

His words snapped me out of my trance, and I attempted another half-hearted twirl. Al and Scarlet were still talking, but it now looked like an argument. He pointed a finger at her, his pale face now red with fury. Al reached into his pocket and pulled something out. I couldn't see what, but I knew something had gone wrong, and the last thing I wanted was to put Scarlet or anyone else in danger.

"We have to act now, Bing. Is everything in place?"

"Yes. We only need—"

Pooky, the drunken elf from the front row, chose that moment to jump onto the stage and try to grab my butt. Since I currently wore nothing but a thong, there was a lot of butt to grab.

I reacted instinctively. Before he could touch me, I kicked him right in the jingle balls as hard as I could.

It had been overkill, and I may have caused some permanent damage, but I had a low tolerance for butt grab-bers. Pooky flew off the stage and landed flat on a table in the front row, in a puddle of spilled eggnog, his hands on his crotch. The whole incident lasted only seconds, but the distraction cost me.

I looked up to see Scarlet standing in the middle of the bar, right in front of Ganja's table, with a triumphant smile on her face and something clasped in her hands. That smile morphed into a confused and horrified expression as she stared at a point behind me on the stage. She seemed to be fixated on the curtain, but I saw nothing out of the ordinary there. I turned back to face her and heard an odd whooshing noise as I felt something fly past my head. My left ear stung, with an odd burning sensation, but I barely noticed. My attention remained on Scarlet.

She opened her mouth, but nothing came out. She locked her gaze on my face as she reached for her neck, her eyes wide with fear. I didn't know what had happened, but I knew it was something terrible. I screamed her name, but before I could react, her eyes rolled back in her head, and she crumpled slowly to the floor.

TWO

Scarlet's head hit the ground with a thud. "I Saw Mommy Kissing Santa Claus" continued playing in the background, but the room had grown oddly silent and still. She lay only a few feet away from me, but I felt frozen in place. As I came out of my stupor, one thought filled my head.

I was about to watch another friend die right in front of me.

My friend Joy had died of a candicocane overdose on the streets of Central City in the North Pole less than a year ago. She'd been given the drug without her knowledge to keep her silent. I knew it couldn't be an overdose this time, but it felt like watching Joy die all over again.

I flew off the stage and ran to Scarlet, searching the sea of faces for my partner, but Bing was nowhere in sight. Instead, I addressed Carrots, the red-headed miner. Carrots seemed the least drunk out of the whole bunch, meaning he still had his eyes partially open and wasn't slumped over the table.

"Carrots. Call for help. Now."

As Carrots pulled his phone out of his pocket and did as

I asked with shaking hands, I knelt next to Scarlet. She lay flat on her back, her red lips abnormally bright in her pale face. Her hands clutched desperately at her neck as an odd gurgling sound came from her throat. A small pool of water was under her head on the floor. Why was there water on the floor? Had she slipped?

"It's okay, Scarlet. Help will be here any minute. What happened?"

She couldn't answer. She opened and closed her mouth, like a fish out of the water. Seconds later, blood spurted out from between her fingers in a gush.

Still on the phone with emergency services, Carrots let out a gasp. "Oh, heavenly hosts. Someone shot her. Someone shot Scarlet."

One of the miners screamed, the sound so high-pitched and jarring it made me flinch. Several of the customers ran for the door, panic etched on their drunken faces. I looked up, frantically searching for Bing. I couldn't contain the crime scene and take care of Scarlet, and I had to take care of my friend. She was in bad shape.

"I've got to apply pressure to the wound. Someone give me a shirt."

At least half a dozen miners immediately took off their jumpsuits and stripped down to their skivvies. Carrots got to me first, handing me his brown uniform with a worried frown on his freckled face.

"Is she going to be okay?"

"I hope so." I applied pressure to Scarlet's wound, but the blood continued to flow out of her with each beat of her weakening heart "Did you see what happened?"

Carrots shook his head. "No, but when she first went down, I thought it might have been another drug overdose."

"This is no overdose," I said, pressing on the wound as

hard as possible without further compromising Scarlet's airway. "It's not stopping. I don't know what else to do."

A sense of profound helplessness came over me. I found myself wishing Jax were here. He would know what to do. He was good in a crisis.

Carrots' uniform, already soaked with blood, wouldn't absorb any more. I noticed Al's handkerchief on the floor and grabbed it to use in addition to the uniform. When I picked it up, a flash drive fell out and clattered to the floor.

My eyes met Scarlet's. She blinked once. I didn't know if that was a message for me or not, but I shoved the flash drive into my cleavage.

Scarlet released a final gasp before her body went completely still. Her eyes stayed open, but no life remained in them. I felt for a pulse, hands shaking.

"No," I said. The word echoed throughout the silent room. Someone had finally turned off the music, thank Santa, but now it felt almost too quiet. I looked around in alarm. "Someone do something. Please."

I nearly wept with relief when the Elven Medical Team arrived and began CPR. Strong hands lifted me and pulled me aside so they could work. At first, I thought it was Bing, but to my surprise, it was Ganja Green who held onto me.

"Let them have some space, *bèl fi*. There is nothing we can do for her now except pray."

He had the singsong cadence to his voice indicative of a nature elf, and I found it soothing. I needed soothing, especially when the EMTs shook their heads sadly and stopped their attempts to bring Scarlet back.

"She's gone," said a female EMT, glancing at her watch. "Time of death—11:30 pm."

"But I don't get it," I said. "There was no sound. No gunshot. She just fell over."

Ganja frowned. "You're right. Why wasn't there a gunshot?" He glanced up at the other elves. "Did anyone else hear or see anything?"

The miners and assembled strippers shook their heads. A few were crying. I felt like crying, too, and my knees were about to give out. If Ganja hadn't held me up, I might have slumped to the floor.

"I don't understand what happened." I looked down at my body realizing I'd ended up covered in Scarlet's blood. I'd knelt in a pool of it, and as I'd applied pressure to the wound, a fine mist had settled on my chest, stomach, and my face. I still sparkled with glitter, and that effect, combined with Scarlet's blood, was macabre.

I fought the urge to whip off the mask and wig and run to the bathroom to scrub myself clean. I needed to be here. I needed to hear what the others had to say. Unfortunately, no one seemed to know what had happened.

I shook my head in disbelief. How had things gone so wrong? Al had slipped away, Bing was nowhere in sight, and Scarlet... poor Scarlet was dead.

Also, the elf I'd kicked in the jingle balls still lay moaning on the table. The EMTs were checking him out, and it looked like he needed medical attention. I'd kicked him harder than I realized. This had turned into a nightmare.

One of the other EMTs covered Scarlet's face with a sheet. "The fifth one tonight. Three overdoses, two murders."

"Two murders?" Multiple murders in one night was almost unheard of on the North Pole.

He nodded, his expression grim. "The other one happened only a few blocks away—a mugging. We'd just brought the body to the morgue when we got the call to come here. Sadly, it's still early. Hopefully, there won't be any more murders, but this won't be the last body tonight. The way so many elves are dying these days for no good reason at all. It's a real crime."

Crime.

I couldn't save Scarlet, and I wouldn't be able to get the information I needed from Al tonight, but maybe I could do something right, like questioning one of the underworld's most legendary criminals.

I glanced up to see Ganja slip into his coat and leave the bar.

"Jiminy Christmas," I said.

The EMT gasped, but I had no time to apologize. I pushed the assembled people aside, most of them hairy, bearded, inebriated miners in their underpants, and ran after the mobster.

That was not my best decision. Ganja had the reputation of being a dangerous man. Secondly, I was nearly naked, and it would be bitterly cold in the back alley of the strip club, but I ran out anyway, hoping I could catch up with him. It didn't take long. I barreled right into him as soon as I opened the back door. He let out an "oomph" when I nearly knocked him over. Fortunately for him, Ganja was a wall of muscle. I was not. He grabbed my arms to keep me from falling.

"Cho!" he said, using the Creole exclamation for surprise. "What's the rush, sweetheart?"

I gazed up at him, once again mesmerized by his face. He had the most intriguing eyes. I'd thought they were brown, but they were actually a deep forest green.

"I'm here to stop you from leaving a crime scene. You're a witness to a murder."

His mouth quirked into a smile. When he studied my

face, however, he seemed to realize I was serious and gave me a puzzled frown. "You truly think you can stop me? Are you crazy?"

My teeth began chattering so badly I couldn't answer him. The chill seeped into my bones, and I had nothing on to protect me from the elements except a push-up bra and a thong that could technically qualify as dental floss. It may have been even smaller than dental floss. No wonder Ganja didn't take me seriously. And the mask on my face was useless as well. The satin made my face feel even colder. Also, Scarlet's blood instantly froze and turned to pure ice on my skin. That made things even worse.

After I convulsed in another full-body shiver, Ganja sighed and looked skyward as if seeking guidance. Pulling off his jacket, he wrapped it around my shoulders, his hands lingering on the lapels. I wanted to shrug it off, but it felt way too warm and smelled good.

Ganja Green was not what I expected, and I seemed to be in a pickle. Bing wasn't around, and Jax had no idea I'd come here tonight. I'd promised him repeatedly that I wouldn't do anything stupid, and this qualified as stupid, but why stop now? I had one of the most dangerous gangsters in the whole elven world standing right next to me.

While I was nearly naked.

In a dark alley.

Covered in blood.

And wearing his coat.

I cleared my throat. "Thank you for the jacket, but I cannot permit you to leave. I'm sure the police will want to question you involving the murder of Scarlet Knickers and—"

"Wait a second." He frowned. "You think I killed Scarlet? Why would I do that? And who are you to ask me such a thing?"

This had been a terrible idea. There had been no room for handcuffs in my thong. Heck, there was barely room for me in my thong.

"I'm, uh, Mistle Ho."

Rats. Why did I say that?

Ganja was not impressed. He lifted one eyebrow. "And you think you can stop me from leaving, Mistle Ho?" he asked. When I nodded, he laughed. "You and what army?"

He ran his big hands up and down my arms to warm me, which seemed nice for a bad guy. He was even taller and stronger than I'd realized. And hotter. He may have been the best looking mobster I'd ever seen.

I gave myself a mental shake. Crap on a cracker. I needed to focus.

Ganja had no trouble focusing. All his attention remained on me as those big hands went up my arms and to my neck. I knew I should have been scared, but I wasn't. I simply stood there like a big dummy. His face was only inches from mine, and I thought he might kiss me for a second. Instead, his fingers dipped into my cleavage, pulling out the flash drive.

"I'll take this with me," he said, his voice low and rough. "*Fu tru.*"

He used the nature elf phrase meaning "believe me." I did believe him, but I couldn't let him take that flash drive.

"Oh, no, you will not." I tried to grab it, but he held it above my head, and the guy was more than a foot taller than me. He shoved it into the pocket of his suit just as a sleek black sled pulled up next to us. It had darkened windows, so I couldn't see who opened the door for Ganja, but he paused before getting into the vehicle.

"Until we meet again." To my surprise, he leaned close and whispered in my ear. "To be clear here, I didn't kill Scarlet. I want you to know that because it's the truth."

With that, he got into the car and took off, leaving me in the alley wearing his jacket and not much else. I turned, planning to open the door to the club and go back inside, but it had locked automatically.

This was not my night.

I planned to trek around to the front of the club, but I heard a commotion, and the door swung open. I jumped back, nearly landing on my butt on the pavement. Another set of hands steadied me. These belonged to the one person I'd hoped would not find me out here like this. My boss. Jax Grayson.

"Hi," I said, giving him a little wave, which looked ridiculous since the sleeves of Ganja's jacket hung well past my hands.

Jax's grip on my arms tightened. "Hi? Is that all you can say?"

Bing came out the door behind him. He had a gash on his forehead and held a napkin there to stop the bleeding. He leaned against the wall with a sigh of relief when he saw me.

"Tink. Thank goodness."

"What happened to you?" I asked, lifting my fingers to touch the wound on his forehead tentatively.

"Someone whacked me on the back of my head. I fell forward, and I guess I hit my face on a table on my way down. I'm so sorry."

"You have nothing to be sorry about," I said. "I'm the one who should apologize."

"You've got that right," said Jax, in all his dark elf glory, an angry scowl on his face. I shivered. This time it wasn't entirely because of the cold. Jax and I had shared a mutual attraction and a few steamy kisses, but we'd both worked hard to maintain a professional relationship since I began working at the EBI. But there was nothing professional about the way he looked at me right now. He acted like he might want to throttle me, but not in a good way.

"Let's go inside," I said, feeling the cold again now that my little adrenaline rush caused by Ganja Green had evaporated. "We need to talk."

"We do," said Jax, his voice clipped and his expression cold. "Because Scarlet Knickers is dead, and it's our fault."

Even though he said "our," I heard what he meant.

Scarlet had died...all because of me.

THREE

I still wore Ganja Green's coat hours later at the police station. My shoes had given me blisters, and my nether regions felt chaffed because of the thong, but all I could think about was Scarlet and the look on her face as she'd taken her last breath. I'd scrubbed my hands and face, but the rest of me still felt sticky with her blood. It was a lot to process.

She'd trusted me, and she'd died because of it. I put my face in my hands. I wanted to weep, but I had to explain things to the Chief of Police, Eve Sleigh. I reported to Jax, and Jax reported to the head of the Elven Bureau of Investigation and Elven High Council. But since I'd involved Bing in this, I'd violated several major rules regarding the chain of command. Chief Sleigh did not seem happy. I could hear her yelling at Jax through the closed door of her office, and I knew I was next.

A few minutes later, her door opened. An athletically built elf with short, gray hair, Chief Sleigh had a temper and a blood pressure problem. I wasn't helping either of those things today.

"Holly," she growled, red-faced and glowering. "Get in here. Now."

With a sigh, I stood up slowly and limped into her office. My feet were killing me, but I couldn't do anything about that now. I had bigger problems at the moment.

Jax wouldn't look at me as I walked in. He sat stiffly in a beat-up leather chair in front of Chief Sleigh's desk. A muscle worked in his jaw, his hands clenched into fists on his lap, and his mouth remained set in a rigid and somewhat judgmental line—all ominous signs.

I stood awkwardly next to him, hovering, unsure what to do. I wrapped Ganja's coat more tightly around my body and waited.

"Sit," said Chief Sleigh, barking out the word and pointing to the vacant chair next to Jax.

I hobbled to the chair and plopped down onto the seat in a cloud of sparkles. I'd discarded the wig and mask but had residual glitter on my hair and body. Now it was all over Ganja's coat and covered Chief Sleigh's office, too. She'd have glitter on her desk and floor for weeks—the nature of the beast. And she'd think of me every time she saw it and get even madder.

This would not end well. I could tell already.

"What were you thinking?" she asked her tone one of barely contained fury. A vein pulsated on her forehead. That was not a good sign.

"I wanted to crack the case...?"

She stared at me in disbelief. "I realize Agent Grayson is at fault for permitting this hair-brained scheme, but according to Nativity Bing, it was your idea. So, I repeat, what were you thinking?"

I glanced at Jax from under my lashes. He hadn't authorized anything, but now he was taking the fall for me, which made it even worse.

"Don't blame Jax—" I began, but he cut me off.

"Oh, I blame myself," he said, sending me a silencing look. "You're right, Chief Sleigh. We instigated a hair-brained, ridiculous, idiotic plan that resulted in the death of Scarlet Knickers and the disappearance of Al Winkle, a valuable informant. Detective Bing got injured, and Agent Holly's cover was nearly blown. Also, Ganja Green somehow ended up on the scene, which compromised the investigation into his activities. We failed on every level, and I accept full responsibility."

I shook my head, more glitter floating around me, but Chief Sleigh held up a hand when I opened my mouth to speak. "I don't need to hear another word, especially from you, Ms. Holly. I appreciate Agent Grayson taking the hit for this, but it's not that simple. We have no shooter. No gun. A missing informant. A mobster on the run. And a dead body. We only needed a fire, a drug overdose, and an intoxicated reindeer or two to complete the picture. Couldn't you have arranged that? I feel like you're slacking."

I didn't bother responding to her question or defending myself. "What happens now?" I asked.

"There will be an investigation into this matter. Heads will roll, and I hope one of them is yours." She gave me a pointed look. "I wish I could suspend both of you, but sadly that doesn't fall under my jurisdiction. However, I can suspend Detective Bing until we sort this out."

"But none of it was his fault," I said.

She folded her hands on her desk. "I realize that, but it's protocol. You should have thought of that before dragging him into this mess."

She was right, and it made me feel even worse. "Is there anything else?" I asked as the total weight of what I'd done hit me.

"I think that's quite enough." She tilted her head to indicate the door, her expression annoyed and angry. "You can leave now."

Jax and I rose to our feet, but Chief Sleigh sent one final order to us before we exited. "And I expect you to clean my office tomorrow, Holly. The place looks like a glitter bomb exploded in here."

I gave her a thumbs up, afraid that if I nodded, it would cause even more glitter to fall, and left her office. As soon as Jax closed the door behind him, I shot him a sorrowful look. "Jax, I—"

"Don't talk to me right now," he said through gritted teeth. "I can't handle it."

He stomped away from me, looking beautiful even when angry. Jax had dark hair, dark eyes, broad shoulders, and a body to die for. He also happened to be an excellent kisser, which I knew from personal experience, and he had a wonderfully dry sense of humor, but he wasn't laughing now. He acted very pissed and justifiably so.

I didn't have a change of clothing in my locker, so I had to wear my stripper outfit, stripper shoes, and Ganja's coat home. Also, Scarlet's blood still covered my body. Thankfully, Ganja's coat hid most of it, but due to the glitter and blood, an Ubersled was out of the question. I had to ride the subway.

It was not a pleasant trip. I got propositioned twice and yelled at by a cleaning crew member for getting glitter all over their nice, clean floor. When the heel broke off my shoe and I twisted my ankle heading up the steps to my apartment, it seemed like the perfect ending to the perfect day. I took off the shoes, my feet aching and my ankle throbbing in pain, but the fun wasn't over quite yet. My roommate, Noelle, waited for me with Bing curled up next to her on the couch. He had a bandage on his head and snored softly. Noelle gently stroked his hair as she glared at me. She didn't even say hello.

"He has a concussion," she muttered, keeping her voice low. "And he needed stitches."

"I'm sorry." I glanced at Bing. "Is he okay?"

She bit her lip. "He will be. The concussion is mild, so I'm letting him sleep, but I'm keeping an eye on him. I'll wake him up and reassess him in a few hours."

"I'm sorry—"

"Don't you dare," she said. "I can't believe you did this. You lied to him. You put him in danger. And for what?"

I leaned against the wall, exhausted. "More people are dying. It's even worse than before. I knew Jax wouldn't jump on it quickly enough, but it was an important lead, and I thought I could crack the case."

"Crack the case? You wanted to be the hero. You like saving the day and getting all the attention. You didn't think about who else could be hurt by this if everything went South Pole, did you? Once again, you jumped in without evaluating the potential consequences, and now others are dealing with the repercussions."

"I said I'm sorry—"

She waved away my apology. "It's not enough. They'll suspend Nat. You realize that, don't you? And Scarlet is dead. You can't fix this, Tink. No one can."

Her words weighed on me. I stared down at my bloody, blistered toes. "Maybe I should stay somewhere else for a while. Give you some space."

"Maybe you should."

I don't know what response I'd expected, but that wasn't it. I inhaled sharply, and the pain hit me full force. Noelle had been my best friend for as long as I could remember. I'd lost many people over the years due to poor decisions and bad behavior, but never her. She'd been my rock, but now I'd lost her too.

FOUR

After I texted Grandma Gingersnap to let her know I'd be crashing with her for a few days, I limped into my bathroom. I was a mess. My feet ached, and, oddly enough, my ear hurt, too. I hadn't noticed it earlier since I'd been distracted and running on pure adrenaline. Now it throbbed painfully and incessantly.

I pulled back my hair and winced when I realized I had a cut on the upper part of my left ear. Like all elves, I had pointy ears. I might have lost the pointed tip if the cut had been less than an inch higher. But how had this happened?

I remembered the whooshing sound I'd heard and the strange burning sensation on my ear but had no idea what it meant. After wiping away the dried blood, I saw the cut was small and would heal well on its own, so I turned on the water and stepped into the steaming shower with a sigh.

The glitter and Scarlet's blood slid off my hair and body and went down the drain in a vibrant swirl of color, and the warm water felt good on my sore ear and battered feet. It couldn't make my heart feel better, though, because I knew Noelle was right. I had wanted to be the hero. I hadn't thought about Bing. I was a lousy detective and an even worse friend. I'd failed once again, and this time I'd done more than screw up. I'd cost Scarlet her life, and I could have also cost Bing his life.

The thought weighed heavily on me. I couldn't fix what happened to Scarlet, but maybe I could improve things for Bing. It might not be possible, but I had to try. I'd speak to Chief Sleigh first thing in the morning when I went to work cleaning up the glitter in her office. Right now, I had to clean myself. If I showed up at my grandmother's house covered in glitter and someone else's blood, I'd never hear the end of it.

I washed my hair, my throat tight with unshed tears, and scrubbed the sparkles from my body. I knew I couldn't get it all, but I did my best. By the time I finished, my skin felt raw, but I was mostly clean, and I'd managed not to cry. I feared once I started, I wouldn't be able to stop.

Noelle probably hadn't meant I needed to leave immediately, but I wanted distance. Even if she had been right, it hurt, and I couldn't deal with another lecture right now.

Stepping out of the shower, I wrapped a towel around my body and dried my hair. Since Noelle and Bing were asleep, I didn't want to use the blow dryer, so I did my best with a fluffy, white towel. I combed it out, pulled it into a tight bun, and dressed in a comfy pair of sweats and a hoodie. Ganja's coat was on my bed, still covered with glitter and a few specks of blood. I dabbed at those, and attacked it with a lint roller, deciding to bring it with me to Grandma Gingersnap's. Returning it to Ganja might give me the chance to talk to him. Even though he said he had nothing to do with Scarlet's death, there were a lot of unanswered questions and warrants out for his arrest all over the elven world.

I cringed when I remembered how I'd confronted him. I'd looked like a total idiot. Chief Sleigh was already pissed at me, but when she found out I'd had Ganja in my clutches and got nothing but his coat in return, she may have a cardiac episode. And if she found out I'd grabbed Scarlet's flash drive as she lay dying on the floor and let Ganja take it from my cleavage moments later because he'd distracted me with his hotness, it could kill her. This was bad, and I had no one to blame but myself.

Tossing some clothes in a duffle bag and slipping into Ganja's coat, I stepped outside. To my surprise, Jax stood on the sidewalk.

"Still wearing that coat?" he asked.

I pulled it more tightly around my body, dreading the upcoming lecture. "What are you doing here?"

"I wanted to make sure you made it home safely." He rubbed the back of his head with his hand. "I tried to call."

The fact that he'd come to check on me made me feel even worse. I glanced at my phone. He'd called several times.

"Sorry. I was in the shower."

"Are you okay?" he asked, his voice gruff.

His kindness nearly broke me, but I lifted my chin and attempted to give him a reassuring smile. "I'm fine. As well as I can be under the circumstances. I'm going to stay with my grandmother for a few days. I was about to grab an Ubersled."

"Noelle kicked you out?"

"Pretty much."

He tilted his head to indicate the sleek, black sleigh parked across the street. "I'll give you a ride."

I thought about refusing, but what was the point? "Thanks," I said, slipping into his vehicle. We drove in silence for a few minutes. When I couldn't stand it anymore, I turned to him. "What do you think will happen tomorrow?"

"It's likely they'll suspend us both. Or worse. But there isn't much we can do about that now."

I put my face in my hands. "Please don't take the blame for me, Jax. It's career suicide."

We'd stopped at a red light. He pulled down my hands and stared into my eyes. "The buck stops here, Tink. Also, you saved my life not long ago. I owe you one."

He referred to the time I'd gotten him out of the burning barn when Sugar and Frank tried to kill us, but he'd saved my life, too. "No. You don't owe me anything."

"Yes, I do. It's part of dark elf culture. A debt I must pay. By taking the blame for this, I'm evening the score." He gave me a crooked smile. "Until I save your life again. Then you'll owe me."

"I already owe you so much."

The light turned green. We drove a few more blocks before turning onto Morningstar Drive, my grandmother's street. It wasn't until we pulled up in front of her place that he finally put the sleigh into park and turned to gaze at me.

"No, you don't, Tink." He paused like he wanted to weigh his words. "We'll talk tomorrow, but I wish you'd been able to trust me. Maybe things could have ended differently if you'd come to me with this."

"I know. You're right. I screwed everything up."

He paused again, and I knew it was too much to hope for, but I wanted reassurance. I wanted him to say it would be okay. He didn't.

"There will be a thorough investigation. Chief Sleigh has notified your uncle. I'll meet with both of them tomorrow. Topper and Finn O'Reilly will be there as well."

Topper, my uncle's head of security, had always been good to me. We went way back. Finn was Jax's boss. An air elf, he was tiny and mean but a brilliant detective.

"Oh, no. Not Finn O'Reilly."

"Yep."

Director O'Reilly worked out of Elf Central, the capital of the elven world, located in a veiled dimension overlapping the city of Las Vegas and invisible to human eyes. Elves from all the elven communities lived there, and it was where all the main government offices were located, including Elven High Council. Jax and I worked for the Elven Bureau of Investigation, the EBI, but the Elven High Council had initially sent Jax to the North Pole to work on the candicocane problem, which was how we'd met. I had been assigned to him in order to keep him distracted. I failed at that job and helped him solve the case instead. At that time, my inability to follow directions had been a plus. This time, not so much. And Director O'Reilly showing up here could be terrible news indeed.

"Air elves are the worst," I said with feeling. "They're biters."

"He's not going to bite you, Tink."

"Maybe not, but he's going to be brutal."

Jax let out a soft chuckle. "Agreed."

Although we were all members of the same ancient, magical species, the elven tribes had several essential differences. Some of those differences were physical, and others had more to do with the chosen professions of each tribe.

Christmas elves like me were happy, sparkling toymakers. At least that was true for the ones living under the biodome on the North Pole. Other elves lived outside the dome. Even though technically Christmas elves, they were different. Known as outliers, they took care of the jobs other

Christmas elves didn't want to do, like coal mining, garbage disposal, and reindeer wrangling, and they often felt ostracized because of it. Although things had changed in the last few years, there was still a lot of prejudice against those living in outlier communities, and I doubted that would end soon. My late mother had been an outlier, but I'd only found that out recently. It had been a well-kept secret my whole life.

Dark elves like Jax were secretive, too, and mysterious and strange. The time they spent living underground lent to their natural pallor and aura of darkness. They usually didn't interact with the other elven tribes, but Jax seemed like an anomaly. I'd never met a dark elf until he showed up at the North Pole and rocked my world (in more ways than one). Although we'd been instantly attracted to each other and indulged in a few hot and heavy make-out sessions, our relationship had become entirely professional once I joined the EBI.

Mostly.

He still wanted to make sure I made it home safely, and his eyes still smoldered when he looked at me, but he'd been strictly hands-off, which sucked. I liked him hands-on. Jax was highly skilled with his hands.

The other tribes in the elven world were nothing like dark elves or Christmas elves. Water elves had gills. They could breathe air but mostly lived underwater. Snow elves lived on the South Pole. Nature elves lived in forests, parks, and jungles. They were the most environmentally conscious tribe—a bunch of hippie tree-huggers who preferred to be naked most of the time.

Ganja was a nature elf but, like Jax, an oddity. He seemed organized and driven. He wore clothing and didn't act like a pothead. In the nature elf community, Ganja Green was a unicorn.

Air elves, like Director O'Reilly, had wings, but they couldn't fly—they hovered. Pretty pathetic. They were the smallest of the elven species, and I hadn't lied. They were biters. My old boss from the reindeer division, Puck, got in a fight with one once and nearly lost a finger. It was ugly.

Jax had to meet with one of them in a few hours, making me feel even worse about what I'd done. The combination of Director O'Reilly, Chief Sleigh, the burly Topper Twinkle, and my uncle (aka Santa Claus) would be quite the gathering.

I glanced up at my grandmother's house with a sigh. Her bedroom light was out, which meant she'd already fallen asleep. I'd have to explain all of this in the morning. It would not be good, but, thanks to me, Grandma Gingersnap had dealt with disappointment involving me many times before. She was used to it at this point.

After my parents died in a freak sleigh accident, I'd grown up here, under Grandma Gingersnap's watchful and slightly judgmental eye. We adored each other, but she'd always been perfect, and I was not, so I made things a bit of a challenge for her. I made things a bit of a challenge for everyone.

I turned back to Jax. "I've already said this, but I am so sorry."

"I know you're sorry," said Jax. "I wish that were enough."

"So do I. Goodnight, Jax."

"Goodnight, Tink."

Waving goodbye to Jax, I walked up the path to the house. I always seemed to end up back here, but I wasn't the only one. I glanced at the home next door to my grandmother's. My ex, Winter Snow, had grown up there. He'd been my first love and (like my grandmother) perfect in every way. His parents were the opposite, however. They'd hated me most of my life and had been part of a plot to kill me that involved my favorite sweets, Snarkleberry Dingalings.

Death by chocolate.

They failed, obviously, but after extensive community service in the outlier community, they left the North Pole in disgrace and moved to Florida. Win bought their house, which made my grandmother ecstatic. She adored Win. Everyone did.

The fact that Win could afford to buy a mansion and I couldn't afford any additional Ubersled rides this month said a lot. We'd started at almost precisely the same place, with the same benefits and entitlement. Win had taken all he'd been given and made a success of himself. I'd taken it and tossed it in the garbage. It was not entirely my fault, but I looked like a spoiled little rich girl to most people who didn't know me but had read about my exploits in the *North Pole Gazette*. I looked like a spoiled little rich girl to those who knew me, too, especially after today.

I used Grandma Gingersnap's key to unlock the front door and stepped inside. I dropped my duffle bag on the floor and headed straight to the kitchen. As expected, she'd left food for me—a sandwich and a plate of cookies. I scarfed them down, still wearing Ganja's coat. I was starving. Pole dancing and being part of a failed police operation took a lot out of me.

After finishing the last bite, I washed it down with a big glass of milk. As Santa's niece, I had a genetic need for milk and cookies. I wiped my mouth with a napkin and tossed it into the garbage. I planned to trudge up the steps to bed, but as I took off Ganja's coat, something fell out of the inside pocket, along with a pile of residual glitter—a business card.

I picked it up and stared at it. It was for a meditation retreat center in the rainforests of Belize, a popular spot for nature elves. On the back, it listed Ganja's name, dates, and the words, "Enjoy your stay."

And for the first time since I watched Scarlet die, I felt the tiniest spark of hope.

FIVE

The following day, I awoke to the smell of sizzling bacon and the sound of voices. Following the scent, I stumbled into the kitchen, still half asleep, and looked up in surprise to see a crowd had assembled. Jax, Win, Topper, and my uncle sat around the kitchen table, digging into plates piled high with bacon, eggs, potatoes, and toast. Grandma Gingersnap, wearing a cheery apron over her perfectly ironed and impeccable clothing, eyed my wrinkled pajamas and messy hair with a frown.

"I figured the bacon would wake you up. Is that glitter on your forehead?"

I rubbed my forehead with the back of my hand as I grabbed a cup of coffee. "It's from the strip club. I must have missed a spot."

The fact that she didn't blink an eye at the words "strip club" showed how far my grandmother had progressed recently. Or maybe it demonstrated how much I'd broken her down.

She pointed to an empty chair next to Jax with her spatula. "Sit." She shook her head in disgust but still put a steaming plate of hot food in front of me. Feeding me was Grandma Gingersnap's love language.

After taking a large bite of scrambled eggs and a swig of orange juice, I glanced up sheepishly at Jax. "Hi," I said softly.

"Hi."

"How bad is it?"

"On a scale of one to ten, it's about a twenty."

Topper agreed with him. "At least a twenty. Maybe even a twenty-five."

My uncle, aka Santa Claus himself, tugged on his white beard, his bright blue eyes concerned. "Which is why we're all here this morning. We need to get this sorted out before we meet with Chief Sleigh and Director O'Reilly this afternoon."

Win lifted his hands. "I'm here for the bacon. Thank you, Mrs. Holly."

My grandmother patted his head like he was ten and not thirty. "You're always welcome here, Win."

Win winked at me. It was a standing joke between us that we thought my grandmother secretly preferred him over me. It made sense. He was the perfect grandson and movie-star gorgeous, with his blond hair and blue eyes. Rumor had it he would be next in line to replace my uncle as Santa when he retired. Win also was one of the nicest people I'd ever met. I'd loved him since I was small, and I imagined I'd always be a little in love with him, but it hadn't worked out between us. We remained close, but I couldn't imagine myself as a future Mrs. Claus, and neither could anyone else.

There had been whispers that I might be next in line for the big job myself, especially after I helped solve the candic-ocane distribution case last year. But I knew that would be a huge mistake, and it seemed everyone else had finally caught on. The debacle yesterday had sealed the deal.

I was exactly what they thought. A one-hit wonder. A fake. A fraud. An imposter. But I still wanted to keep trying, which made me something else as well.

A total idiot.

Win got up, kissed Grandma Gingersnap on the cheek, and patted my shoulder. "Good luck today."

"I'll need it," I said, waving as Win left. I turned back to the others with a sigh. "Not only will there be an internal investigation, but I also have to find a way to get all of the glitter out of Chief Sleigh's office this morning." I shook my head as the weight of it hit me. "I'm elfing screwed. That woman has a lot of crevices."

My uncle laughed but grew silent when my grandmother sent him a withering look. "Don't you dare 'ho, ho, ho,' at this, Kristopher. It's not the time. We've enabled this ridiculous behavior for far too long. I had a path of glitter up my steps this morning. Like a happy trail straight to Tink's bedroom."

Jax choked on his eggs. I patted his back. "Sorry," he said, taking a sip of water.

"Not your fault."

He glanced at me. "What happened to your ear?"

I reached up. Although still sore, it was already healing. "I'm not sure. It happened at the club. I felt a sting, and kind of a burning sensation, but I didn't realize I'd been cut until I got home. I guess I was a little distracted."

Topper sat back in his chair. "Distracted? I wonder why."

He teased, but his words held no judgment. A former reindeer wrangler and professional skier, Topper and I had always had a special connection. He'd been the first one on the scene after the sleigh accident that took my parents when I was a little girl. I'd somehow come out of that horrible incident emotionally traumatized but physically fine. Everyone called it a miracle. Since my middle name was, in fact, Miracle, it seemed like a sign of great things to come. Sadly, I hadn't lived up to those expectations. The only miracle was that I hadn't died due to a poor decision on my part.

Yet.

My uncle poured more coffee into his cup, adding several spoonfuls of sugar and a dollop of fresh cream. When he sipped his coffee, he got cream on his white beard. Grandma Gingersnap dabbed at it with a napkin. Once a mother, always a mother. He thanked her with a twinkle in his blue eyes and turned back to us.

"What is our next step?" he asked.

"Today, we'll meet with the group and launch the investigation," said Topper, brawny arms folded over his chest. Even though he was my uncle's age, he still had the body of an athlete, with a flat stomach and broad shoulders. He was not a cookie eater, and he took his coffee black. He tilted his head to study me, his dark eyes intense. "Is there anything else we need to know before we step into that room, Tink?"

I'd planned to tell him about the card from the meditation retreat center but changed my mind. Although Jax had asked me to trust him, I knew what he'd say if I told him I planned to crash Ganja Green's meditation retreat and get that flash drive back. It was a risky move, but the only chance I had to make things right. I had to take it. I had no idea what might be on the flash drive Scarlet had given me, but I knew it had to be important, too.

Jax's phone rang. He excused himself and took the call. We sat eating breakfast in silence until he returned. I reached for more bacon, but I stopped as soon as I saw the look on his face.

"What is it? What happened?"

He shoved his phone into his pocket. "The coroner's office called. They have a cause of death for Scarlet Knickers."

"Well, isn't it obvious? Someone shot her, right?"

His eyes met mine. "There was no bullet. We scoured the club. There is an entrance wound in the front of her throat and an exit in the back, but both are tiny. The coroner's best guess is someone stabbed her, but the knife they used had to be at least eight to ten inches long and the width of a needle. A very sharp, very long needle. They pierced both her external carotid artery and her internal jugular vein."

The bacon and eggs churned in my stomach. "No, I watched her go down. She was standing in the middle of the bar alone. I never saw a knife. I would have noticed a knife—especially one that was nearly a foot long. And I would have noticed a stabber too. It never happened."

"Maybe and maybe not. Think back to what happened, Tink. Was anyone else nearby?"

I closed my eyes and tried to picture the moment Scarlet went down. Reliving it felt painful, but I had no choice. I touched my ear.

"They're wrong. It had to be a bullet, Jax. Something zipped right past my head. I heard it. And I think maybe it grazed me."

He swallowed hard. "It grazed you? But there was no bullet, Tink, and no one heard a gunshot. Is that correct?"

I nodded. "Yes. No one heard or saw anything."

Jax pushed back my hair to better study the cut on my ear. "So what caused this?"

Topper frowned. "Maybe it wasn't a bullet. Just something moving fast. A different sort of projectile."

"A projectile?"

"Exactly. Or it could have been a retractable knife. You might not have seen that, Tink. Or maybe something else. You'd be surprised what's out there. We used lots of crazy weapons when I was in special operations for the United Elven Army."

"Hold on. When were you in special ops?" I asked.

"Before you were born," he said. "During the ogre wars. The one time all elves teamed up to truly work together for the common good. I had elves from all the different communities in my platoon. South Polars. Air elves. Nature elves. Water elves. And dark elves like you, Jax. We united against a threat. I'm still in touch with some of them, even today. Finn O'Reilly was one of them. We go way back. I'm looking forward to seeing him today. I wish it could be under better circumstances, but that always seems to be the case with Finn and me. The last time I saw him was at his wife's funeral, which was awful."

"And now this whole mess," said Grandma Gingersnap. "Poor Scarlet dying for no reason and with no suspect and no murder weapon. It's so cruel. So cold."

"It is, but I think Topper has some interesting theories," said Jax. "What else can you remember, Tink? Who was at the club?"

"There were four other dancers there that night. They were all backstage."

Jax took a notepad out of his inside jacket pocket and read over his notes. "Four other dancers? Are you sure? Because only three were there when the police arrived."

I frowned. "I'm sure."

"Could you identify the three that were there and tell us who might be missing?"

"Maybe. We were all masked. And I was focused on not messing up the operation and not breaking my neck while pole dancing in a thong."

"By all things festive and holy..." muttered Grandma Gingersnap, closing her eyes. My uncle patted her hand comfortingly.

"What else do you remember, Tink?" asked my uncle. "Was anyone else backstage?"

"The announcer, but I didn't see him. The props guy. He was masked, too."

"What happened next?" asked Jax.

I struggled to picture the area and remember details, but I could only see Scarlet's poor face as whatever it was hit her neck. I bit my lip and forced myself to focus. "I went onstage, and Scarlet approached Al Winkle. They spoke, but only for a few seconds. She walked away from him and stood in the middle of the room, right in front of me. She looked...happy. But then her expression changed. She seemed to be staring behind me, but there was no one there. Just the curtain in the back of the stage."

"Who else was close to her?"

"Ganja Green sat at a table a few feet directly behind her. No one else was around."

"And the thing that went past your head, the thing that hit your ear, came from the back of the stage?"

"Yes. It must have. I mean, that's how it sounded. But there was no one there. I looked. Then I turned back to Scarlet, heard a whoosh, and she went down."

Jax touched my wound, his face paler than usual. "It certainly appears as if you were grazed by something. If you'd moved, even an inch, in the wrong direction..."

His voice trailed off. I swallowed hard. Grandma Gingersnap sank into a chair, visibly shaken. "You could have died. Oh, Tink."

My uncle patted her shoulder. "But she didn't die, Mother. She's here right now."

"And Scarlet isn't." I shook my head in disbelief. "I got there in seconds, but it was already too late. How could I have missed it? I didn't see anything or anyone suspicious, and I was standing right there."

"Stop beating yourself up. The coroner told me no one could have saved her. Whatever the weapon, it was a kill shot. They knew exactly what they were doing."

My mind raced. "Didn't Scarlet have cameras in the club?"

Jax leaned back in his chair. "She did. State of the art. But they'd been disabled."

"Someone planned this," said Topper. "And it doesn't sound like the work of an amateur. I think a professional is responsible."

"You think it was a hit?" Tears swam in my eyes. I blinked them away and cleared my throat. "But who would do that, and why would someone want to kill Scarlet Knickers?"

"That's the big question," said Jax. "And it's up to us to find the answer."

<h1 style="text-align:center">SIX</h1>

Even though I'd only spent a few minutes in Chief Sleigh's office the day before, it looked like a glitter bomb had exploded inside. "Jiminy Christmas," I said. "This is going to take all day."

"You're right," said Chief Sleigh, breezing in behind me. "And watch your mouth."

I jumped. "Sorry." I wore yoga pants and a hoodie, and my feet still ached from the shoes I'd worn while pole dancing. My inner thighs felt chaffed, too. Whoever thought a sequined thong was a good idea should be pelted with snowballs in their nether regions for an eternity. Although, to be honest, snowballs on my crotch might feel good at the moment. I glanced warily at Chief Sleigh, who looked like she wanted to pelt me with more than snowballs.

"Should I start now or later?" I asked, putting down my bucket of soapy water and tossing a sponge inside. I had several rolls of paper towels, too. I'd tried various methods for glitter removal in the past but found the old standby of soap, water, and wiping worked best. Strange, yet true.

And the fact that I knew different glitter removal techniques said a lot, but I'd had a complicated relationship with it since I was a little girl. I'd always loved the sparkle, the same way a squirrel was attracted to shiny objects, but I usually regretted it later—like the night of my senior prom. I'd thought sprinkling glitter in my hair would be a fantastic idea. Win, my date, got some of that glitter in his eye, and we had to go to the emergency room. We returned in time for the senior committee to crown him prom king, but he had a bandage over his eye in all the photos.

Reason number 541 his parents hated me. Or it may have been 542. It was hard to keep track.

"Now," said Chief Sleigh. "Thanks to you, I have to meet with Director O'Reilly today and launch an internal investigation."

"Because of Scarlet's murder," I said, swallowing hard.

"And because of Ganja Green. We'd been tracking his activities for the EBI, but you blew the whole investigation. He's gone now, and that slime bucket Al Winkle is gone, too."

I considered telling her about the meditation retreat but held back. Instead, I tucked my hands into the pocket of my hoodie. "I assume Director O'Reilly will suspend me as you conduct the investigation."

She laughed. "I'd say that's a safe assumption."

"And I deserve it, but Bing doesn't. It's my fault, not his."

She gave me a steady look, her blue eyes as hard and cold as ice. "Our actions have consequences. Bing should have known better. He didn't follow the chain of command."

"But he's new. He only recently started this job."

"He's a good cop, and he knows there are rules. You might be protected by your family and by the EBI, but Bing is not. Someone has to take the fall, and it isn't going to be me."

Her words made me ill. "That isn't fair."

She snorted. "Welcome to real life, princess. Clean up my office. I want all traces of you removed from this place. Are we clear?"

I nodded, unable to speak. She grabbed her briefcase and stomped out of the room. I didn't tell her she had glitter covering the seat of her pants. That would have made things worse.

CLEANING the office was painstaking work. The glitter wedged itself in between the planks of the wooden floor. It covered each surface. It took forever to get rid of it. Every time I thought I'd finally finished, I found more.

I left the files on Chief Sleigh's desk for last. I figured the best thing to do would be to shake them off carefully and scrub the desk. But as I shook the first file, something interesting fell out—an address for Al Winkle's mom.

Al's father had been a Christmas elf like me, but his mom, Petunia, was a nature elf. She lived on a commune in the nature elf community and grew pot for medicinal purposes. I frowned as the wheels turned in my head. Al might be our prime suspect. He'd been standing close by, and he'd been the last person to speak with Scarlet. When Al disappeared, he could have gone to stay with his mother. The place was remote enough that he might feel safe there.

Checking first to ensure no one watched me, I jotted down the address and shoved it into my pocket. Maybe I'd visit Petunia after I went to the meditation retreat to find

Ganja. I'd be killing two birds with one stone if Al were there.

The door flew open, and Chief Sleigh marched in, her face nearly purple with fury. I jumped guiltily away from the desk, and she growled at me. "Enough, Holly. No matter how hard you clean, the glitter will keep showing up. It's a lot like you."

"Excuse me?"

Jax hovered in the doorway, his expression grim. "May I?" he asked. When Chief Sleigh nodded, he entered, closing the door softly behind him.

Chief Sleigh flopped into her chair, and Jax stood near the window. No one said anything. I picked up my bucket, looking like a scullery maid. "Should I leave—?"

"Sit," they both said at once.

I lowered myself into the chair directly across from Chief Sleigh. From this vantage point, I could see both of their faces and knew something had happened. Something bad. And they had no idea what to do about it.

Maybe this meant they weren't going to fire me. If they had decided to give me the axe, Chief Sleigh would have been dancing on her desk right now.

A sharp rap sounded at the door. Neither Jax nor Chief Sleigh seemed surprised, and I realized we'd been waiting for someone else to join us.

"Come in," barked Chief Sleigh.

The door opened, and in fluttered Director O'Reilly, head of the Elven Bureau of Investigation and my boss. Well, he was technically my boss's boss since Jax reported directly to him. I knew him by reputation alone. Despite his diminutive size, he was brilliant, bold, and a little scary.

It made me think of the difference between a big dog, like a golden retriever, and a small dog, like a chihuahua.

Sane people would realize that even though the retriever might weigh eighty pounds and the chihuahua four, it made no difference. The chihuahua was the dangerous one, like Director O'Reilly.

He glanced around the room, his feet a few inches above the ground. He wore a brown suit with unique cut-outs in the back to accommodate his wings. They were iridescent and sparkly, a total mismatch to his stern face and wire-framed glasses. He had a handlebar mustache, and his mouth, barely visible beneath the mustache, was set in a hard line.

I jumped to my feet, knocking over the bucket of dirty glitter water in the process. It poured over the once clean floor of Chief Sleigh's office, making it worse than it had been in the first place. When I lurched forward to pick up the bucket, I slipped in the water and knocked over my chair. They all watched me as I righted the chair and the bucket. My cheeks burned with humiliation.

"I see your reputation was not exaggerated," said Director O'Reilly, his voice oddly soft and reedy. I'd never spoken with an air elf before. Maybe they all sounded like that. I had no idea.

"I'd like to apologize for what happened—" I began, but he cut me off with a shake of his head.

"Please don't. There is nothing you can say that will make any of this better. You've made Chief Sleigh appear incompetent and Detective Bing seem like a fool. Oh, and you've also made Agent Grayson look like an idiot for hiring you in the first place and permitting a situation to unfold that required my inter-vention. Luckily for you, I was already here for a meet-ing, but because of you, I had to stay an extra day. I hate the North Pole, and I hate Christmas. And I hate that there is nothing I can do to make all of this go away."

I nodded, finding it hard to swallow over the lump in my throat. "I'll offer my resignation effective immediately."

"No."

I looked up at him in surprise. Even though he was tiny, since he floated six inches above the glitter-soaked floor, I had to tilt my chin to make eye contact with him. What I saw there made a shiver of worry go over me.

"What do you mean?"

"I mean, I won't accept your resignation. You've embarrassed the department and your family. You messed this up, and now it's up to you to fix it."

I frowned. "How?"

"Ganja Green will open a new casino in Atlantic City next month. This gives us a unique opportunity. According to witnesses, he thinks you're a stripper, and you made some sort of connection with him. We're counting on that being true. We want you to go back undercover so we can catch him. At last. But if you screw this one up, you're out."

I gaped at him, shocked. "I'm grateful, but I don't deserve this."

"You're right. You don't. Giving you another chance was Topper Twinkle's idea, not mine. I would have you fired. But being the niece of Santa has its advantages."

Jax and Chief Sleigh both averted their gaze, and I knew, in that instant, they agreed with him. I expected that from Chief Sleigh, but it hurt coming from Jax. I wanted to crawl into a hole. I cleared my throat.

"I think Al Winkle may have had something to do with this. He was the last person to speak with Scarlet. He had motive, means, and opportunity."

"And he seems to have disappeared off the face of the

Earth," said Chief Sleigh. She tapped a pencil on her desk. "What was his motive?"

"Scarlet blamed him for her daughter's death. She was convinced it was more than an overdose and felt certain someone else was involved as well. She wanted answers. She'd become obsessed with it, and she thought Al held the key. He knew something. She was sure of it."

"That's motive," said Jax. "If Al wanted to silence her."

Chief Sleigh glanced at her notes again. "But why was Ganja Green there? Did Al owe him money? Because lots of nature elves owe him money."

"It's possible," I said. "I don't know."

Chief Sleigh rubbed her temples. "And what about means? If Al killed Scarlet, how did he do it?"

"I'm not sure. It's possible he may have had a weapon, and I just didn't see it. The opportunity for him to use it occurred when I got distracted. A miner tried to grab..." I paused, not sure how to describe it. "Something he shouldn't."

Chief Sleigh glanced at her notes. "A miner? Do you mean someone named Mr. Pooky T. Bear, by any chance? Because you crushed one of his testicles when you kicked him last night. He had emergency surgery and lost a jingle ball. He's going to sue the department."

"Oops."

"Oops?" asked Chief Sleigh.

"Well, he tried to grab my—"

Director O'Reilly rolled his eyes. "This is nonsense. We need to focus on how to deal with Ganja Green next month."

Chief Sleigh gave him an odd look. "I can do both. I have a case to solve here. I'm capable of multi-tasking."

"If you say so," he said, disgusted. He pointed a thin

finger at me. "Until we figure this out, I want you off the grid. You're on unpaid leave for the next three weeks. I don't want to see you or hear a word about you that entire time." He turned to Jax. "The same goes for you, Grayson. You've been an outstanding agent, but we all have a weakness. I thought I knew what yours was, but I guess I was wrong. If you aren't careful, it will destroy everything you've worked for." His gaze shot to me, his expression dismissive. "And it's not worth it. Trust me."

He left, fluttering out of the room, his wings buzzing like a bumblebee or a hummingbird. "Well, at least he didn't bite us," I said, hoping to ease the tension in the room a notch. It didn't work.

"He's had a rough couple of years," said Chief Sleigh, her voice tinged with exhaustion. "Give him some slack."

"What happened?"

"His son died in a freak accident five years ago. He was their only child. His wife couldn't handle it and killed herself last year."

"Oh, wow. That's awful. I didn't know."

"How could you?" asked Chief Sleigh. "Director O'Reilly doesn't broadcast his personal issues for all the world to see. He does his job, which is what we should all be doing. So, get out of here. Now."

"There is one last thing," I said, swallowing my hurt pride. "Last night, the EMTs said Scarlet's was the second murder of the night. I don't know if there is any connection or not, but I thought I should tell you."

Chief Sleigh picked up a pile of papers and began leafing through them. "Last night?"

"Yes. According to the EMTs, it was a block away from Sugarbum's."

She ran her finger down the page. "Oh. Here it is. The

victim was stabbed and robbed a little before 10 pm. They identified the body this morning. His name was Gus Gravy, but I don't have any other information. Do you know him?'

"Yes." I glanced at Jax, my hands shaking. "Gus Gravy was Scarlet's prop guy. I saw him last night at around eleven. He gave Scarlet a can of glitter so she could spray me."

"THE GLITTER that is all over my office right now?" Chief Sleigh rubbed her temples again. She seemed to be getting a migraine. "You saw him at eleven? You must have your times wrong. He was killed at ten."

"No, it was eleven. I'm sure of it. So that means it seems pretty likely that someone killed Gus and pretended to be him at the club."

"Wouldn't Scarlet have noticed?" asked Chief Sleigh.

A shiver went over me. "It was Halloween. We all had masks on. The fake Gus Gravy had dressed as Quasimodo. He wore a full face mask and a cloak with a hood. No one would have known it wasn't him."

"She's right," said Jax. "It's too strange to be a coincidence. The fake Gus has to be our killer. That changes everything."

Chief Sleigh looked skyward. "Will this day never end?" She took out her notepad with a sigh. "I guess I'm not getting rid of you quite yet, Holly. Start from the beginning. And this time, tell us the whole story."

SEVEN

After telling her (almost) everything that had happened the night before, I took my bucket and left Chief Sleigh's office. The one bit of information I omitted had been about the flash drive. The last thing I needed was Chief Sleigh to have another reason to get mad at me.

And I didn't tell her about the meditation retreat Ganja planned to attend. I kept that a secret as well. But Jax eyed me carefully like he knew I was holding something back. He followed me out the door when I left.

"Tink, we need to talk."

"No, we don't. I get it. I'm a failure and a disappointment. I ruined the whole investigation. There is no need to tell me all that again. Chief Sleigh and Director O'Reilly communicated it quite clearly."

While you stood there, saying nothing.

I didn't add the last part, but I thought it. He had valid reasons to doubt me, and it shouldn't have hurt so much, but it did. With a muttered curse, he grabbed my arm and pulled me into an empty conference room. He didn't turn on the lights. There was nothing inside but a metal table, a few chairs, and a sad-looking wreath hanging on the wall. It was depressing. On the North Pole, wreaths were mandatory adornment for any bare space, but this one felt like an afterthought. It made me sad.

When Jax leaned close and I noticed the dark circles under his eyes, I felt even more miserable. I wanted to cry but forced myself to speak.

"This is not at all what I intended. Not for me. Not for you. Certainly not for poor Scarlet."

"I know."

The fact that there was no judgment in his tone, only a sort of weary resignation, made tears prick behind my eyes. It took everything I had not to dissolve into a sobbing heap. But Jax kept me steady. I wasn't sure how or why he did it, but he balanced me somehow.

He had a file in his hands. He put it on the table and inside were photos of three women.

"These were the three dancers at the club when the police arrived. Do you recognize them?"

I nodded. "That's Cinnamon," I said, pointing to a blond elf with dark skin wearing gold. "And those are the twins. I don't know their names." The two redheads were identical and wore black. They'd danced together, mirroring each other precisely. Freaky and yet mesmerizing.

"Who is missing?"

I frowned. "The girl in blue. She had dark hair and a rose tattoo on her butt. She went on right before me. I didn't know her name, but she was gorgeous. Well, from what I could tell."

"Since you all had masks on." Jax took notes. "Anything else?"

"No." I shook my head. "Some people left the club after Scarlet went down, because we all thought there might be a shooter. Most came back, though, to give a statement. If the dark-haired dancer didn't return, where could she have gone?"

"I have no idea." After glancing toward the door, he placed his hands on my shoulders and spoke softly. "Listen, Tink. Something is going on here. I'm not sure what it is. I have to figure it out. Can you please do as Director O'Reilly asked and lay low for a few weeks? I'd ask you to avoid trouble, but that would be pointless. Try to be safe, okay?"

The worried expression in his eyes made me pause. "What's going on, Jax?"

He shrugged; his gaze shuttered. "I'm not sure yet. It could be a gang war that's brewing. Why was Ganja at that club in the first place? That's not his usual routine. Betting? Yes. Smuggling? Definitely. Strip clubs? No. They aren't his style."

"Al seemed surprised to see him there."

Jax nodded. "And that's another thing. According to Bing, something spooked Al. Yes, he was probably shocked to run into Ganja Green, but I feel like there is more to this story. I don't understand their connection yet, and I need to figure it out." He ran a hand through his hair. "I mean, after my suspension is over. Until then, my hands are tied, and each moment we lose could be the difference between figuring this out or more people getting hurt or killed. But I have no other options."

"What will you do?"

"Go back to Elf Central. Research what I can about Ganja and Al. Try to see a connection. Find out the name of the missing stripper. Figure out how a dead man gave you a can of glitter. And do it all under the radar. What about you?"

"The same," I said, unable to make eye contact. "I might

go away for a few days. Get out of town. You know, go some-where that I can think."

"Not your grandmother's house?"

I gave him a wry smile. "Definitely not there. And I'm not sure when Noelle will let me move back in. It's better if I take off. She needs time, and I need to figure out a way to make things right between us."

He placed a hand on the side of my neck, cupping my face with his palm as he stroked my cheek with his thumb. "Be careful."

"I will," I said. "You aren't mad at me?"

He stared at me, his eyes scanning my face. It seemed like he might kiss me for a second, but no such luck. He took a step back.

"I'm furious. But I still care about you. No matter what idiotic thing you do, I can't seem to stop." He studied my face, his expression serious. "Director O'Reilly was right. You are my weakness. But he was wrong as well."

"About what?" I asked, still a little dazed. Jax did that to me.

"You are worth it, Tink. Even if you drive me crazy, even if you make poor choices, even if you lack any common sense at all—"

"Hey—"

He put a finger on my lips to silence me. "You are worth it. And although I regret what happened, and I often hate the choices you make, I don't regret you. Don't change that, okay? Don't make me regret you. Because I have little left."

He walked out the door, and I watched him go, confused by his words, but my resolve to fix this felt stronger than ever. I had to do this. I couldn't bring Scarlet back, but I had to make things right. Unfortunately, there was something else I had to do first.

After showering and changing my clothing back at my grandmother's place, I jumped in an Ubersled and went to the North Pole Home For Elderly Elves. I grabbed a bouquet from the gift shop in the lobby, got the room number for Scarlet's mother from the reception desk, and went to her room. I wasn't sure what to expect since Florina Dazzlethighs was a legend in the exotic dancing community, but what I saw when I entered her room shocked me.

A little old lady sat primly on the bed, wearing a pretty, red housecoat. She was wide awake, but the second occupant of the bed, an elderly gentleman elf, snored away peacefully, completely naked. I knew because his bare bum greeted me as soon as I walked in the door.

"Oops. Sorry," I said, covering my eyes. "I'll come back later."

"No need, pet," she said, with a strong Cockney accent. "Time for Bubby to leave anyway."

"But Ms. Dazzlethighs—"

"It's fine. And call me Flo. Everyone else does." Flo shook the man's shoulder. "Bubby. Wake up. You need to go back to your room now, love."

"I do?" he asked groggily.

She kissed him loudly on the forehead. "Yes, darling, but you can come back later and finish."

"Okay."

Bubby got up, naked as a jay bird, and stepped into his slippers. He started to walk out the door. Flo stopped him. "Don't forget your robe, pet. You don't want to get into trouble again for flaunting your prized possession."

He chuckled. "You're right," he said, grabbing a robe off the hook by the door and putting it on. "You're always right. That's why I love you."

He blew her a kiss before leaving. She sighed as she

watched him go. "He loves me because I put out. Then again, so does everyone else in this place. It's a well-kept secret, but the elderly are incredibly promiscuous. And why shouldn't we be? Our days are numbered, so we may as well enjoy them while we can. And he was here to comfort me, poor soul. He forgot in the middle of it and fell asleep." She met my gaze. "Are you here about my sweet Scarlet?"

I handed her the bouquet, a lump in my throat. "Yes, I am."

She lifted the flowers to her face and inhaled deeply. She was beautiful and looked decades younger than her eighty-five years, but the sadness and pain in her eyes broke my heart.

"The police came to see me earlier. Someone named Bing? A handsome thing. The poor boy cried when he told me, but I didn't cry. I'm too angry to cry because a child shouldn't die before her mother. It doesn't matter the child's age. But Scarlet lost Ruby only months before I lost Scarlet. Now both are gone, one to drugs, and one to gang violence. Only my son remains. Oddly enough, he was always the naughty one. Scarlet and Ruby were so good."

"You have a son?"

"Yes. His name is Red."

"Scarlet and Red?"

"Crimson is my favorite color," she said with a smile. "And both of my babies had red hair, so it fit. Ruby had red hair, too."

"What's Red doing now?"

"He's an accountant. But he lives far away, and I never see him."

"Oh." I tried to process that and couldn't imagine Scarlet or Flo being related to an accountant.

"I'll miss my beautiful daughter and granddaughter. I

feel like I should be weeping, but I can't seem to do it. Is it strange that I'm not crying?"

I shook my head. "There isn't one way to grieve. My parents died when I was small, but I didn't cry either. I showed my grief by rebelling. By making my grandmother's life more difficult. I can see it now. I didn't see it then."

She patted my hand. "You poor thing. Were they murdered, too?"

Her words made me pause. It was an odd question. "Uh, no. It was an accident."

"I see. That's terrible. Someone murdered my Scarlet."

"I know," I said. "I was with her when she passed."

She studied me more carefully. "You're Tink Holly?"

"Yes."

"Scarlet told me about you. She said you were friends." Flo squeezed my hand, her grip surprisingly strong. It had to do with all the pole dancing. If you couldn't hold on, you'd be in trouble. As I stared down at our clasped hands, Flo continued speaking. "I'm glad you were with her. I'm glad she wasn't alone."

I closed my eyes, fighting a flood of guilt and pain. "It was my fault. We were trying to get information on who may have given those drugs to Ruby. Scarlet was helping me. I put her in danger."

Flo shook her head. "It was her choice. If she wanted to do something, there was no stopping my Scarlet."

"But I was the one who planned it. I was in charge."

"Did you shoot her?"

"No, but—"

"Then you aren't the one who killed her, but I trust you to figure out who did. Scarlet trusted you, Tink, and so do I." She patted my hand. "So put aside that guilt, love. Move on and give an old woman some peace. Make her death count for something. Make her daughter's death count, too. Make this better. Make this right."

I promised her I would, but I knew the truth. Making this right meant going behind Jax's back, and Chief Sleigh's, and Director O'Reilly. It also meant lying to my grandmother, my uncle, Topper, and Noelle, but I had to do it.

"I will," I said. "And I'll do one better. I'll make them pay."

"Good," she said. "But there is one more thing you have to do first." She paused. "You're going to have to take care of Scarlet's cat."

EIGHT

Mr. Pussypants hated me from the moment he laid eyes on me. It got worse when I shoved him in a cat carrier and brought him to Grandma Gingersnap's house. By the time we arrived, we were both a mess. I was covered in scratches, and he crouched in his cage, hissing with hackles raised. I couldn't unlock the front door while holding the carrier, so I rang the bell. Grandma Gingersnap answered with a frown on her face.

"What fresh hell is that?"

I held the carrier up higher. "Mr. Pussypants. Your new roommate."

She lifted her hands and marched to the kitchen. "Nope. No way."

I followed her. "Please. It's only for a few days. I swear. Until I find him a home." I paused. "His owner was murdered. It was my fault."

She let out a frustrated groan. "And you're going to force me into caring for him because you feel guilty?"

I bit my lip. "Well, kind of. I couldn't leave him. And I have to go out of town..."

"So you're dumping him here? Why can't he stay with Noelle?"

"Our apartment doesn't permit cats. Also, she isn't speaking to me."

"She isn't speaking to you?" Grandma Gingersnap let out a long sigh. "She must have her reasons."

"She does."

"And there is no one else?"

"Not really. Lots of people aren't speaking to me at the moment."

Mr. Pussypants let out another hiss. Grandma Gingersnap pointed to the laundry room. "Put that poor animal in there, let him out of his cage, and shut the door. Do you have a litter box?"

I stared at her blankly. "Uh, no."

"Food?"

"Also, no."

She looked skyward, and I knew she was counting to ten. "Put the cat in the laundry room, make him as comfortable as possible, and don't take off your coat. We're going shopping."

<hr>

AFTER A TRIP to the pet store that took far longer than I expected, we arrived home with our arms full of supplies, only to find that Mr. Pussypants had shredded Grandma Gingersnap's favorite cashmere sweater while we were out. Not a good start. He stared blankly at us when we poured dried cat food into a bowl.

"Maybe he doesn't like this brand," I said.

Grandma Gingersnap, still pissed about her sweater, let

out a huff. She went to the kitchen, grabbed a tin of tuna, and opened it for the cat. After giving her some serious side-eye, he delicately tasted one bite, then another.

"Wow. You're the cat whisperer."

She glowered at me. "Don't try to flatter me. He is beautiful, though, with all that long, gray fur and those big, beautiful blue eyes. What did you say his name was?"

"Mr. Pussypants."

She put a hand on her chest and shook her head. "I will not call him that. You'll have to think of a new name."

"Mr. Pussy?"

"No."

"Clawed DePussy?"

"No."

"Pussy Galore?"

"No," she said, and this time she looked concerned. "There is something seriously wrong with you."

"Fine. I don't know. We could call him Cat. Or Bob."

She crossed her arms over her chest. "Cat is too unimaginative, and he's too beautiful to be a Bob."

"How about Knickers? After Scarlet Knickers. And because right now, your knickers are in a twist."

"You're ridiculous. No. Not knickers. But something relating to Scarlet would be nice." She thought about it a second before her face lit up. "I've got it. He should be Rhett. He's Mr. Rhett Butler."

I gazed at her with admiration. "That's perfect."

"It is," she said. Mr. Pussypants, now known as Mr. Rhett Butler, rubbed against my grandmother's legs lovingly. When I reached down to pat him, he hissed at me and tried to swat me with his razor-sharp nails. I jumped back.

"Settle down, buddy. I can still return all those toys we bought you. I mean it."

"You'll do no such thing," said Grandma Gingersnap, picking up Mr. Rhett for a snuggle. She kissed his head before setting him in the bed we'd purchased for him. He stared at her adoringly. She patted his head before turning to me with a stern look. "We're going to have a nice long talk. Now." I took off my coat, and she noticed the scratches on my arms with a shake of her head. "After we take care of those. Poor Mr. Rhett. You must have upset him."

In typical Grandma Gingersnap fashion, she'd somehow found a way to blame me for the scratches all over my arms. But she covered me in antibiotic ointment and tiny bandages and made me sit at the kitchen table with a cup of cocoa and a plate of cookies. This would not be punishment for most people, but she didn't put marshmallows on my cocoa, so I knew I was in trouble.

"Tell me exactly what is going on, Tink. I mean it."

I opened my mouth and closed it again. "It's complicated."

"I don't care."

"It's a police investigation."

"I have top security clearance."

This surprised me. "You do?"

"I'm Santa's mother. That gives me certain privileges. And I'm your grandmother. After everything you've put me through, I think I deserve a little honesty, don't you?"

She made a good point. "Fine, but you have to swear you won't tell anyone. And you have to promise you won't try to talk me out of it." I thought of something else. "Oh. You also have to let me borrow your clothes."

Grandma Gingersnap had the best clothes, and we wore the same size. I always went to her closet when I needed something classy, and she knew it. She just didn't like it very much. She narrowed her eyes at me.

"Start talking, Tink."

After taking a long sip of cocoa, no marshmallows (sad, sad cocoa), I told her everything. It felt good to get it off my chest. She knew some of it following the meeting at breakfast, but she didn't know about Ganja, the flash drive, or the meditation retreat. I showed her the card.

"I know this place," she said. "It's very high-end. And they have a great spa. But it's pricey, and reservations are hard to come by. How will you get in?"

"I'm going to do what I swore I'd never do," I said, rubbing my temples as a dull headache took root. "I'm dipping into my trust fund, and I'm going to drop the Holly name."

She sat back in her chair, stunned. She knew exactly what it took for me to hit this level of desperation. I didn't even do it when I was falsely accused of a crime and imprisoned in the coal mines last year.

"It's really that important to you?"

"I screwed up," I said. "I thought I was doing the right thing, but it turned into a disaster, and my friend died because of it."

She folded her arms over her chest. "And what do you plan to do when you encounter Ganja Green at the retreat?"

I took another swig of cocoa, but it was cold at this point and even sadder. "I'm going to get the flash drive back. Nothing more. And full disclosure, if he doesn't give it to me willingly, I'll steal it."

Grandma Gingersnap covered her face with her hands. "Oh, Tink. This will not end well."

I pulled her fingers down from her face. "Yes, it will. Do

you know why?" When she shook her head, I continued. "Because I have a plan. Because I know what I'm doing. Because I've met Ganja already, and he seems oddly reasonable for a criminal."

She groaned. "I don't know about this. Maybe we should tell your uncle."

"Please don't. It's better for him if he doesn't know. Plausible deniability. But I'm telling you because you asked and because I trust you. Also, as I said already, I have to borrow your clothes."

She studied me, and her expression was wary. "Will you call or text me every day?"

"Yes."

"Will you be careful?"

"Yes."

"Will you contact Jax the minute you feel like you're in over your head?" I was about to tell her I wouldn't, but she stopped me. "Either you promise me that, or I'm calling Topper now."

I lifted both hands in surrender. "Fine. I will reach out to Jax if things get dicey, but that won't happen. I've learned my lesson, and I'm not trying to save the day. I'm trying to right a wrong. My wrong. Please let me fix this."

There was a long silence. The only sound was the faint hissing of Mr. Rhett Butler coming from the laundry room. Grandma Gingersnap stood up. "Fine," she said as she picked up my empty mug. "You can borrow my clothing. I won't tell anyone where you're going. And I'll even make the reservation for you at the retreat center but take a little extra cash out of that trust fund when you go to the bank tomorrow."

"Why?"

"Because you owe me for the sweater that feline destroyed. And I expect to be reimbursed for my cat sitting services."

She was dead serious, so I rose to my feet and gave her a nod. "It's a deal."

NINE

I slipped into my first-class seat on the flight to Belize, and the flight attendant immediately handed me a glass of perfectly chilled champagne. This was a new experience for me. Yes, I'd traveled first class with my grandmother growing up, but I had strict rules about making my way in the world and wanted to prove I could do it. Unfortunately, I'd failed, and those rules seemed stupid and pointless.

The plane, an Airsleigh 57, was a sleek, modern vehicle with over a hundred passengers. I lounged back in the comfortable leather seat, wearing a white suit I borrowed from my grandmother, and a faux fur stole. I'd also gotten my hair and nails done and decided I could get used to this. I'd had access to my trust fund since I'd turned twenty-five but never wanted to touch it. I'd hoped to donate that money to charity. Now I was a charity—not that anyone would contribute to a lost cause like me.

I let out a sniff and forced myself to pull it together. At this point, I'd fallen deep into pity-party mode, but what happened in that strip club had changed the game. Whenever I wondered if I might be doing the right thing, I pictured Scarlet's face as she lay dying on the floor of her brand-new club. I saw the pain and devastation in Flo's eyes. I even remembered Scarlet's stupid, grumpy cat, Mr. Pussypants, aka Mr. Rhett Butler. Scarlet loved that cat, even though he was pretty much a jerk, and she'd loved me, too. She had such a big heart. And she had been a good friend.

I couldn't deal with the pain right now. I was in a public place and needed to keep my head in the game. I'd let myself grieve later after I found Scarlet's murderer and ensured he received the punishment he deserved. Maybe then everyone would forgive me. Maybe even Jax would forgive me.

I remembered the look of disappointment and frustration in his dark eyes and sighed. No, I wasn't counting on Jax's forgiveness. I didn't deserve it.

I glanced at my phone to see the texts I'd gotten from Scarlet over the last few months. I scrolled down to the one she'd sent the day after Ruby died.

My baby is gone. I knew she was going down a dark path and hanging out with the wrong crowd, but I never thought it would end here—with her dead from a drug overdose at the age of twenty-six.

Ruby had been younger than me. It made it worse somehow.

Ruby was an artist. A gentle spirit. And she was an innocent soul. I did what I could to protect her from the realities of this world. Maybe I did too much.

I skimmed through the subsequent texts. I'd told her how sorry I was in my responses, but I wished I'd said more. I scrolled until I found the text I'd been seeking.

I blame Al Winkle. He knows who's involved. He knows where the drugs came from, but he's scared. Someone powerful is involved in this. That's why I'm coming to you for help. Not the North Pole bozos. Someone needs to get justice for my daughter.

Rereading her words made me emotional. Poor Scarlet had been through so much. She shouldn't have died on the floor of her club for no reason at all. But her words chilled me.

Someone powerful is involved in this.

Feeling tears well in my eyes, I shut off my phone. I needed to calm down, and I needed to think. As I sipped champagne, I gazed around the cabin. The plane seemed pretty full. The only empty seat was the one right next to me. The flight attendants, all air elves, fluttered about, helping passengers get settled, but the door to the plane hadn't closed yet. It seemed like they were waiting for someone. I'd requested a refill on my glass of champagne when Ganja Green stepped onto the plane.

"Jiminy Christmas," I said under my breath.

His eyes scanned the first class section. When they landed on me, I thought I saw a flash of recognition in their green depths, but it was gone before I could be sure.

"I believe this seat is mine," he said, his voice deep and low and with the same sing-song cadence I remembered.

I smiled at him, trying hard to remain calm. "Since there aren't any other seats left, I think you're right." I lowered my voice and gave him a conspiratorial look. "Little known fact, if you sit down, they give you champagne."

I lifted my glass to him, and he grinned. "Then I should sit."

As he settled in his seat, I tried to still my racing heart. We clinked glasses when the flight attendant brought more champagne and told us to prepare for takeoff.

"Cheers," I said.

"Here's to a wonderful trip."

We sipped our champagne in silence for a moment. Ganja's arm brushed against mine. If I got lucky, maybe he'd have to use the restroom, and I could rifle through his things, but that might be too risky. The idea that the flash drive from Scarlet might be in the overhead compartment was nearly too tempting to resist, but I held myself back. I needed to be smart about this. I tried to imagine what I'd do in this situation if I didn't know Ganja was a mobster and I wasn't secretly stalking him to get information regarding my friend's murder. We taxied down the runway, and the plane lifted off, leaving the snowy North Pole behind us. I turned to him with a smile.

"Business or pleasure?"

"Both," he said. "How about you?"

"Escape." When he laughed, I continued. Jax had taught me that the key to good undercover work was sticking as closely to the truth as possible, so I gave it a shot. "I'm getting away from some problems at work, problems with my roommate, and problems with my grandmother."

"That sounds like a lot of problems," he said.

"You have no idea."

"Are you heading to the beach? Belize has some gorgeous beaches."

I shook my head. "I'm going to attend a meditation retreat in the rainforest. I thought a little mindfulness might go a long way right now. Also, they have a nice spa."

He eyed me curiously. "You're going to Rockwood Pond?"

I feigned surprise. "You're familiar with it?"

He leaned back in his seat. "Yes. I'm going there, too."

"No way." I grinned at him, pretending I didn't already know that. I settled back in my seat. If I couldn't get the flash drive from him under the watchful eyes of the flight attendants and the other passengers, I reminded myself that I might be able to get it from him at the resort. It was easier since we'd kind of become friends. He knew me now, and the man would have to leave his room sometime.

We chatted about the amenities offered by the resort, and a few times, I caught Ganja sending me an odd look. "Is something wrong?" I asked before waving to the flight attendant for yet another glass of champagne. They were small glasses, and the champagne was excellent. Also, I hadn't eaten breakfast. Champagne on an empty stomach might not seem like a good idea, but it was oddly satisfying.

"Nothing is wrong," he said, eyeing me again. "You look familiar. Have we met before?"

The flight attendant brought refills for both of us, along with lunch. I shrugged as I unrolled the silverware and put my napkin on my lap. "We haven't officially met yet at all." I extended my hand. "I'm Tink."

He took my hand in his. It was large, warm, and strong, and an odd ripple washed over me. Not the same tsunami of sensations I felt whenever Jax touched me, nor was it the comforting wave of emotion I felt with my ex, Win. This was different, a strange little flutter, but it was still something significant.

Why, oh why, did I always go for the bad boys?

"I'm Ganja," he said. I saw the wheels turn in his head as he connected the dots. "Wait. Are you Tinklebelle Holly? Santa's niece? The socialite?"

I nodded, unsure where this might be going and wondering if I'd ever been called a socialite. "Guilty as charged."

"I saw your photo in *Elf* magazine a few years ago. It was an article about your family."

I wrinkled my nose at him. "That was an awful photo. I looked like a beached whale. You read *Elf*?"

Elf was a celebrity gossip and fashion magazine attempting to be something more by adding a few articles but failing miserably. I read it primarily to find out the news about my former friends and colleagues. I'd had a lot of jobs and a lot of former friends and colleagues. I was on good terms with some people I knew from the past, but the list seemed to be shrinking rapidly.

Topper had once said I was an acquired taste, and he may have been right. Not every elf liked me. Many seemed to hate me on sight, but not Ganja.

"You looked beautiful," he said. "I mean, you are beautiful."

I felt my cheeks grow hot. "You're a smooth talker, Ganja."

"No, I'm honest. I never lie. And I prefer not to be lied to as well." He gave me a pointed look. "Are you truly here on vacation, Tink? Because I read the *North Pole Gazette*, too. I know you work for the EBI. And I'm assuming you know who I am as well."

"Ganja Green, notorious gangster?"

He laughed. "Is that what they're calling me?"

I shrugged. "Maybe. What I'm calling you is the guy who happened to sit next to me on my flight to Belize. Yes, I know who you are, but I had no idea you would end up sitting next to me on this plane until you arrived. I'm not traveling for work. I'm not on the clock. No one from the EBI even knows I'm here. And that is the truth."

He studied me closely. "Fine, then. We are two strangers who met on a plane. Nothing more and nothing less."

I wasn't sure if he was trying to give me a message with

that comment or not, but I glossed right over it. "Exactly. But back to that notorious gangster part, I can't believe you read *Elf.* You don't seem like the type."

"First of all, I stopped all that gangster stuff years ago. I'm a legitimate businessperson now. Secondly, I read what I like." He pulled a glossy copy of the magazine out of his bag. "Don't judge a book by its cover, Ms. Holly."

I held out my hand, and he gave me the magazine. As I began leafing through it, I saw a photo of Angelica Frost, my old high school arch-nemesis, a former Miss North Pole, Miss Elven Worlds, and Miss Christmas Spirit. Ganja had dog-eared the page. In the photo, she wore an apron and was ladling soup to homeless elves in the capitol. The caption said something about Angelica being on the short-list for Volunteer of the Year. I let out a laugh that sounded a bit like a cackle.

"Speaking of lies...this elf is a liar if I ever knew one."

He looked over my shoulder at the photo. "Angelica Frost? I understand she does quite a bit of charity work."

I handed him back the magazine. "Only when it suits her. She's a prize whore."

He choked on his champagne. "Excuse me?

"She's addicted to winning. And prizes. And beating others. Trust me, I know. We went to high school together. She is not a nice person. Do you know what you said about books and covers? Angelica has a beautiful cover, but what's inside is a different story. Inside is dark."

He studied Angelica's face in the photo. She had glossy, black hair, bright blue eyes, and a heart-shaped, delicate-looking face. She dressed like a runway model and was built like one, too, but with more curves. Externally, I could agree Angelica was perfection. But she was also one of the cruelest and most selfish people I'd ever met.

"People change," he said. "Are you the same person you were in high school?"

I considered his question. "Pretty much. And that's why I'm going on this retreat." I decided to change the subject. "Wow. This salmon is amazing. Do we need more champagne?"

By the time we reached Belize, I was toasted, and Ganja and I had become buddies. I liked him. It was unexpected, and I didn't want to lie to him, but I had no choice. I needed answers. The list of people I'd hurt was growing by the day. And my list of questions was increasing, too.

Who killed Scarlet and how? Who killed Gus, the prop guy, and pretended to be him at the club? What had happened to the dancer with the rose tattoo? Where was Al?

The answers all seemed to lie with Ganja Green, which was why I was here, spending my trust fund elf bucks on first-class tickets and a stay at a luxury resort. I had to act like honey to catch a bee, even if I hated honey. Even if I'd been avoiding honey my whole life. Even if I knew that honey, for all its sweetness, was nothing but bee vomit.

Well, technically, at least. A beekeeper might argue the fact, but regurgitation was regurgitation in my book. But I was willing to do it if it took pretending to be bee vomit to catch a murderer. I was ready to do or be anything.

TEN

One of the flight attendants flitted over to us as the seatbelt light went on overhead. "Please buckle up. We'll be landing shortly."

She had the same reedy voice as Director O'Reilly. It was definitely an air elf thing.

I glanced out the plane's window at the blue waters and sandy beaches below. It looked like paradise. Even if I was here for less than happy reasons, I could appreciate the beauty of this place.

"It's gorgeous," I said, smiling as I glanced at Ganja.

"It's home," he said, returning my smile with one of his own.

We parted ways as we exited the plane. "I have some things to do before I head to the resort. Will you be alright getting there on your own?" he asked.

"I'll be fine. See you later, notorious gangster."

I gave him my hand. To my surprise, he lifted it to his lips and kissed it. Who knew he was such a gentleman?

"Thank you for a most enjoyable trip, member of the EBI. You were a delightful travel companion."

Flustered, I pointed at him and winked in an overly exaggerated way. "And so were you."

I wanted to crawl into a hole. Why did I point and wink at him? What the holly jolly hell was wrong with me?

Fortunately, he seemed to find it charming because he tossed back his head and laughed. "See you soon, Ms. Holly."

"Bye." I gave him a weird little wave. It was terrible but not as bad as that wink, and as soon as he turned and left, I whacked myself on the forehead. "Jiminy Christmas. What is wrong with me?"

I thought I'd spoken softly, but apparently, I had not. Two nuns from a cloistered nature elf community stood right next to me. They both let out a gasp of surprise.

"Sorry, Sisters," I said, making the sign of the cross at them. I may have done it backward.

Fudgity fudge cakes.

I needed to get out of here before I embarrassed myself again.

The elven airport, located close to Belize City, was tiny and chaotic. After I grabbed my suitcase from baggage claim, I noticed a young elf with dark skin and closely cropped hair who stood a head taller than the crowd. He wore a navy blue suit and held a sign with my name on it. When I approached him, he grinned and bowed at me.

"Ms. Holly? Welcome to Belize. My name is Amyris Branch. I'll be driving you to the Rockwood Pond Resort today. May I take your bag?"

"Sure," I said, pushing my wheeled suitcase toward him. "Thanks."

"No, thank you," he said with a wink. "And congratulations."

Before I could ask him why he congratulated me, he

began walking briskly toward the airport exit, chatting the whole way. I kept up as best as possible in my heels, sweating in the tropical heat. Although stylish and warm on the North Pole, the faux fur stole felt heavy and oppressive here. I took it off, shoving it into my carry-on. I took off my suit jacket, too, and felt better once I was down to nothing but pants and a silk tank top.

Amyris showed me to a sleek, black, floating limo parked by the curb. He helped me in, opened a small bottle of chilled champagne, and handed it to me with a glass.

"Oh, great. More champagne."

"Is it not to your liking? We have whisky, too. And juice."

I immediately felt terrible. "No. This is perfect. I love champagne. Thank you. It's just that I had it for breakfast this morning."

He chuckled. "Well, that's not good, Ms. Holly. But there are some snacks in the mini-fridge. Help yourself."

"Thank you."

I texted Grandma Gingersnap to let her know I had arrived. She responded with *WTF*, which she still thought meant, "Well, that's fantastic." I giggled. It was even better than when I told her LOL meant "Lots of love," and she used it on a sympathy card.

So sorry to hear about the loss of your dear sister. LOL. Gingersnap.

It took her a long time to forgive me for that gem. The WTF lie seemed relatively harmless in comparison.

I put away my phone and sipped champagne as I nibbled on crackers, cheese, and fruit that had been thoughtfully prepared and placed in the mini fridge. The champagne was cool and refreshing in the Belizean heat. I drank some water, too. The last thing I needed was to arrive at the resort wasted.

We drove about half an hour, floating above the city. Amyris pointed out various places along the way. "The resort is located next to the Mayan ruins of Altun Ha. Is this your first time here?"

"Yes," I said, staring out the window at the palm trees swaying in the breeze.

"You'll love it. It's gorgeous. In addition to the meditation center and spa, you can visit the ruins, take a shuttle to the beach, or even watch the human tourists through a special viewing window." He shook his head, laughing. "Humans. They are hilarious."

Like the limo, the resort was invisible to human eyes. We'd learned early on that interacting with the earth's human population meant trouble for everyone involved, especially us. We'd been called fairies at one point in history and leprechauns at others, but some called us things like brownies, dwarves, gnomes, hobgoblins, pixies, gremlins, sprites, and even trolls. Humans were famous for seeing what they wanted to see, and the veil between our worlds kept us safe.

However, we did enjoy spying on them for entertainment. We also tried our best to keep them from destroying the planet we shared, but we led separate lives, occupying the same spaces but on different dimensional planes.

I had never been good at physics and couldn't explain the mechanics of how the veil worked any more than I could explain how the internet worked. It was elf magic. Pure and simple. Why even try to understand?

"You can also visit the rainforest. There are a million things to do," he said, pulling up in front of the resort entrance. I'd read earlier that the architects who'd designed it had wanted to make it look like part of the Mayan ruins surrounding it, and the result was both harmonious and surprising. Amyris turned back to smile at me. "I'm sure you'll have fun, and you won't regret choosing Rockwood Pond for this special occasion."

He hopped out of the limo and opened the door for me before grabbing my bag from the trunk. "Special occasion?"

Amyris studied my face for a moment, before he burst out laughing. "Oh, Ms. Holly. You are a kidder. If you need a ride while you're here, this is my card."

He gave me his business card, and I attempted to tip him. He lifted his hands in surrender. "No, ma'am. It's been taken care of already. Enjoy your stay."

I watched him drive away, perplexed. Things got more confusing when I entered the hotel. Some beautiful nature elves sang a welcoming song for me while sprinkling the path with rose petals and congratulating me. They were all naked. That was a bit of a shock. And when I reached the front desk, I was greeted again with congratulations, more champagne, and more nakedness.

"Welcome to Rockwood Pond," said the receptionist, a pretty elf named Fern. She wore her nametag on a floral lei hanging around her neck, but she had nothing else on her body. "And welcome to Belize. I understand congratulations are in order. Everyone at the resort would like to extend their warmest wishes to you."

"Uh, thanks," I said, no longer bothering to ask why they were congratulating me. I chalked it up to some kind of cultural difference between Christmas elves and nature elves. We were always wishing people a merry everything. Maybe nature elves congratulated people randomly. It didn't make much sense, but I was tipsy from the champagne I'd indulged in today. I was in a happy cloud of bubbly, alcohol-induced joy.

Fern gave me a wristband. "Keep this on at all times," she said. "It's how you get into all our facilities, and it's also how we track you."

"Track me?"

"It's easy to get lost in the jungle, Ms. Holly. We wouldn't want that to happen now would we?"

"No, we wouldn't."

She bowed. I bowed back, and she congratulated me again. I congratulated her in return, and she laughed.

"Be safe. Follow the rules. Keep that wristband on and have a wonderful time."

By some miracle, I managed not to say, "You, too." I was pretty tipsy at the moment, and it took all my focus not to stare at the employees' private parts. There were bare boobies and ding dongs everywhere.

This may have been why when the (naked) bellhop gathered my things, I didn't notice at first that we were following the signs for the honeymoon suite. I trailed after the bare bellhop, smiling the whole way, enjoying the songs of the birds, the smell of the flowers, and the feeling of the warm, moist air on my skin.

It was hot here. Maybe being naked wasn't a bad thing. Tomorrow, I'd deal with Ganja, but today I planned to relax and breathe and possibly get naked. It sounded like a good plan. A great plan. I also wanted more champagne, or maybe a rum punch or a watermelon daiquiri. I'd read about Belize on the way here, and the watermelon daiquiris were supposed to be excellent. I saw one in my future.

I was confused about why they'd assigned me to the honeymoon suite but decided it was a lucky mistake. I gasped when I saw it. The place was beautiful, a luxurious treehouse overlooking the Mayan ruins. I had the option to climb the twisted wooden steps that curved around the tree trunk and led up to the room, or the bellhop offered to hoist me up via a giant swing. I naturally chose the swing, and he hoisted my suitcase, too. I thanked him, waving down at him from the treehouse like a princess. He congratulated me—of course—because all the elves here congratulated me.

"Congratulations, Ms. Holly. I wish you many happy and fruitful years."

"Fruitful?" I asked. He gave me a cheery wave. The people here were all so friendly. Even if they were naked and kept congratulating me for nothing, it didn't matter. I loved this place.

The room was circular, with huge, open windows and a panoramic view. White, filmy curtains fluttered in the breeze, and the sound of music floated in the air from somewhere in the distance. I tried to identify it and realized it was Brukdown, a style of Belizean music that told the story and culture of the people of this country. I closed my eyes and let it wash over me. It was perfection.

I placed my purse on the nightstand and flopped down on the massive bed. Someone had covered the bed with red rose petals. I picked one up in confusion and studied it. I felt drunk, tired, and emotionally drained. That's why it took me a few minutes to realize that I heard something strange coming from behind a door on the far side of the room.

The shower. It was running. Someone was in here with me.

"Jiminy Christmas," I said under my breath, sitting up so quickly my head spun.

As I searched for a weapon, the shower stopped. I sat on the bed, frozen with fear, unsure what to do next. And when the door opened, and I saw who stood there, I realized my worst nightmare had come true.

Jax Grayson. In all his dark elf glory. He had a towel wrapped around his slim hips, water dripping from his dark hair, and a stern expression on his handsome face. He was both hot and bothered.

"You've arrived. At last. Let's get to work. We've already wasted enough time."

ELEVEN

"What are you doing here?" I asked, sputtering in surprise.

"Dealing with you, of course."

"How did you get here before me?"

"There are private jets."

I frowned. "You have a private jet?"

This was yet another layer in Jax's many layers of mystery, and I wanted to know, but he gave me a condescending shake of his head. "Unimportant. It was not hard to figure out where you were going, Tink. You left a trail a mile wide. You bought the tickets in your name, used your credit card, and weren't exactly secretive about any of it." He paused, hands on his hips, and I took a moment to admire the view. He had a lean physique, chiseled abs, and broad shoulders. He was nice to look at, even if he was annoying and snarky. He lifted one finger. "Also, I had an informant. An inside operative."

I rolled my eyes and flopped back down on the bed. "Grandma Gingersnap."

"Yes."

That explained a great deal. "No wonder she didn't put

up a fight. She planned to make you babysit me all along, didn't she?"

He gave me another condescending look. He was good at giving me those, something else he had in common with my grandmother, but Jax had almost elevated it to an art form.

"She thought it wise that I accompany you on this foolhardy mission, and I happened to agree with her."

"You always agree with her. You're in cahoots."

He lifted a dark eyebrow. "Cahoots? Perhaps. But I prefer to think we both have your best interests at heart. And keeping you alive and in one piece is in your best interests. And in ours."

I sat up and folded my arms over my chest, partly relieved he was here and partly furious. "Fine. But I was trying to keep you out of this. If things don't go well, I'll get fired. Or killed. Or worse."

"What could be worse?" he asked, sitting on the bed next to me.

"I'll have to deal with my uncle. But I've disappointed him so much already. What's one more debacle?"

"What's one more debacle?" He lifted his hands in an exaggerated motion. "Wait. That should be your new mantra. It suits you. And since we're at a meditation retreat, you need a new mantra."

His comment made me smile. It also made me feel terrible. "I'm sorry."

"Because you didn't tell me that you knew Ganja Green would be here and may have inside information pertinent to our case? Yes, you should have," he said. "But why trust me now?"

"I do trust you, Jax. It's complicated."

With a groan, I put my face in my hands. He pulled my fingers away from my face and stared at me.

"What's going on?"

I gazed into his dark eyes. "I don't trust myself. I know I'll screw up, and it's like a self-fulfilling prophecy."

I flushed remembering all the times I'd made poor choices. Like when I'd decided wearing a wraparound skirt in middle school had been a good idea. The tie had gotten caught on the doorknob of my homeroom, and I'd flashed the whole class.

Or in college when I'd gotten drunk, snuck into Santa's workshop, and painted mustaches and genitalia on all the baby dolls. I'd used permanent marker. The elves had to work overtime and still couldn't make up for the lost inventory. There were lots of disappointed children that year.

And later when I'd gotten fired from job after job and no longer had the respect of my friends and colleagues. I'd become a joke. After years of missteps and bad decisions, I'd lost faith in my ability to make good ones. Although many of the things that had happened to me weren't my fault, many were, and Jax understood that probably better than anyone.

"I can't help you with that, Tink, but I can help you with something else. Your cover. You gave your actual name when you made the reservation here, which was a rookie mistake. I had to think on my feet, but I came up with something that might work."

"What?"

He waved a hand to indicate the room. "This."

"Oh, no," I said as things clicked into place. The honeymoon suite. The naked people congratulating me. The rose petals all over the bed. "You said we're here on our honeymoon, didn't you?"

"Yes, I did. Congratulations, Tink. Or should I call you Mrs. Grayson now?"

I shook my head, hoping to clear it and find a way out of this. "Uh, Jax. This could be a problem."

He shook his head. "No, it's the perfect cover. Many elves come here for their honeymoon, especially those who want privacy. A Christmas elf from one of the most famous families in the elven world would want privacy, especially if her newly betrothed is a dark elf. Imagine the scandal."

"Oh, I can imagine it. Trust me. And the cover is a great idea, but I'm not sure it'll work."

"Why? Because I hate Director O'Reilly's plan. Wait until Ganja is in Atlantic City and figures it out?" He shook his head. "No. This makes so much more sense. We'll pretend to be a couple and attend the meditation sessions together with Ganja. It'll give us a chance to get closer to him, and maybe we can develop a connection and figure out why he was in the club that night. Maybe we'll also figure out why Director O'Reilly was eager to put you in Ganja's path next month. A lot doesn't add up here, but this will work. I'm sure of it."

"It would work, except for one small thing," I said, hating to drop this on him. "I already got close to Ganja Green. I sat next to him on the flight here. He doesn't seem to realize I'm Mistle Ho, but he does know I work for the EBI. I admitted that I knew who he was as well. I told him I was here on vacation. Since I didn't know about this plan, I never mentioned that the vacation was my honeymoon. Won't that seem odd?"

He ran a hand through his damp hair. Jax needed to get dressed. I wasn't sure how much longer I could sit next to him when he had on nothing but a towel and not touch him. A girl only had so much self-control. I was debating whether or not it might be weird to kiss his shoulder when Jax spoke.

"No. Because we're trying to keep our nuptials hush-hush. That's why we traveled here separately and are being low-key about it. We don't want the paparazzi to find out. We're private people. And between my family and yours, that would be understandable."

"Your family?"

He ignored my question and rose to his feet. "I'm going to get dressed, and I imagine you'd like to shower. We have dinner reservations in an hour. Can you be ready?"

I tilted my head and studied him. "That depends."

"On what?"

"Will you get me a watermelon daiquiri?"

"Is that seriously all you're concerned about?"

"At the moment, yes."

He sent me a smoldering look. "I'll get you two."

JAX WAS a man of his word. As we sat on the outdoor balcony of the resort restaurant, I sipped my second watermelon daiquiri with a contented sigh. It far exceeded my expectations, as did the hotel. Every inch of it was perfect. Jax seemed perfect, too. It was easy to pretend we were here on our honeymoon. I couldn't have chosen a better or more romantic location. Even my dress, a long, white, filmy sundress, fit the mood. I sighed in contentment.

"This is perfect."

"It is." He reached into his pocket. "But I almost forgot."

He pulled out two rings. One was a simple silver band, and the other was a giant diamond surrounded by tiny diamonds. He placed the diamond on the ring finger of my left hand and put the plain band on his.

"What's this?" I asked.

"We have to look the part if we're going to play the part."

I gazed down at the diamond in shock. "This is beautiful, and it looks so real. Where did you get it?"

"It is real, and I had it at home. Please don't lose it. It's a family heirloom, and my mother would kill me if anything happened to it."

"No," I said, shaking my head and trying to hand it back to him. "Absolutely not. You can't trust me with something like this. It's too valuable."

He'd never mentioned his mother before. It made me curious, but I held back. If he wanted to tell me later, he would. But there was no way I could wear this ring. I began to take it off my finger, and he stopped me, covering my hand with his.

"I do trust you, Tink. You won't let anything happen to it. I know you won't."

His words nearly brought me to tears. I didn't deserve his trust, but I could see there was no arguing with Jax over this. "Fine. I'll do my best. I'll keep it safe." I tilted my hand back and forth, gazing at the beautiful ring. Unlike a typical diamond, it seemed to have fire in its depths. I couldn't stop staring at it. Jax smiled.

"You like it, don't you?"

I held it up to the light. "Duh. It's the most beautiful thing I've ever seen. It must be a trick, but it looks like it's glowing from the inside."

"It's not a trick," he said, taking my hand in his so he could also study the diamond. "It's a rochtar diamond, found only in one special mine deep underground. Only dark elves have access to it. We live in such inky blackness. We're always searching for light."

I blinked at him, surprised to hear the sadness and longing in his voice. Also surprised he was talking about dark elf stuff at all. Jax usually didn't share, but I'd heard about his mother, a secret mine, and his desire to find light in the darkness in this single conversation. It was a lot. He seemed to realize it, too. As he released my hand, he acted almost embarrassed. I decided to change the subject.

"So, what do you think of the rum punch?"

He decided to forgo the watermelon daiquiri and had a spicy rum punch. Jax didn't share my love of anything and everything sweet. It was a significant difference between our two tribes, but only one of many.

He lifted his glass. "Taste it."

I took a sip and sighed. "I love the daiquiri, but this is like Belize in a glass. The sea, the sun, the sand, and the jungle. All of it."

"I agree."

I stared into his dark eyes. "Thank you, Jax. For following me here. For trusting me with your ring. For giving me another chance. I hate that we're in this situation, but there is no one I'd rather be in a situation like this with than you." I wrinkled my nose. "Did that make sense?"

"It did. And I feel the same, Tink. You drive me mad at times, but I know you have my back, and I have yours. And I always will."

His words were a soothing balm to my battered heart. "Here's to us," I said, lifting my glass and clinking it with his. "For better or for worse."

He lifted a dark eyebrow. "Let's hope it's for better because it cannot get much worse."

I giggled, and he grinned, and all felt well again in my

world. The trees swayed above us as monkeys frolicked and birds sang. The servers had clothing on, as did the other diners. I was happy not to watch naked people eat. I felt happy in general, and it was as much about the company as it was about the setting.

Jax picked up a hibiscus blossom from the table, tucked it behind my ear, and laced my fingers with his. I gazed at him dreamily but immediately realized his focus was now on something else entirely.

"Ganja just came into the restaurant. Directly behind you. And he's not alone. Is that Miss Elven World on his arm?"

Although I knew I should have been more subtle about it, I couldn't stop myself. I swung around in my seat and realized Jax was right. Ganja had walked in with none other than Angelica Frost on his arm.

I thought about climbing under the table and sneaking out of the restaurant, but it was too late. They'd already spotted me. Ganja smiled and gave me a nod of his head. Angelica's pretty blue eyes narrowed into slits and her perfect little nose wrinkled in distaste.

Our job had gotten one hundred times harder. And Jax had no idea.

"Jiminy Christmas," I said. "We're screwed."

TWELVE

As Ganja and Angelica headed straight toward us, I downed my watermelon daiquiri so fast I got brain freeze.

"Ow, ow, ow."

I knew a trick to combat it that involved putting my thumb on the roof of my mouth. I decided not to attempt it and instead rode the wave of pain. I was still wincing when they arrived but tried to play it cool.

"Heyyyyy," I said, smiling in a way that I felt certain looked more like a grimace.

"Tink Holly," said Angelica. "What a delightful surprise."

Her smile didn't look like a grimace but did not reach her eyes. Oh, no. Her eyes were as mean as I remembered.

She leaned close to give me an air kiss. I caught a whiff of expensive perfume and evil intentions. Well, I smelled the perfume. The intentions were simply something I knew lurked inside her.

"Hi, Angelica. Hi, Ganja. I didn't realize the two of you knew each other."

I gave Ganja a pointed look, and he bit his lip as if to keep from smiling. "We're old friends."

"Not that old, Gan-gan," said Angelica with a flutter of her eyelashes. "We've only been together a few months—a few perfect, wonderful months."

I tried not to gag. "Gan-gan?" I asked, fluttering my eyelashes at him. It didn't have the same effect since mine were not as long or as fake as Angelica's.

"It's my special name for him." She looked up at him adoringly before turning her attention to Jax. "Tink and I went to high school together. We go way back. Who is your friend, Tink?"

"Jax Grayson. He's my..." I froze. We hadn't gone over this yet, and I didn't know how to introduce him.

Jax chuckled. "It's okay. You can say it, sweetness." He took my hand and kissed the back of it before addressing Angelica and Ganja. "I'm her husband. We're recently married. We want to keep it hush-hush since we haven't made a formal announcement yet, but we're here on our honeymoon."

"Oh," said Angelica, her gaze immediately going to the giant rock on my finger. "Does Win know?"

Odd question, but she'd known Win in high school, too. I stared at her, once again not sure how to proceed. Jax saved me.

"No one knows. We eloped. We plan to surprise everyone with the news when we return."

She only paused a split second before gushing over the announcement. "Well, congratulations. I'm so happy for you. And we won't tell anyone. Your secret is safe with us."

"Thank you," said Jax. "Would you like to join us for dinner? It would be nice to get to know one of Tink's old high school buddies."

"Are you sure?" asked Angelica. She tried to act polite, but I could tell she was eager for more gossip.

"Definitely," said Jax, moving to sit in the chair next to mine. Ganja and Angelica sat across from us. "Isn't this nice?"

"Fantastic," I said with a tight smile. "Two EBI agents, a notorious gangster, and a beauty queen walk into a bar, and…"

I heard Ganja smother a laugh and resisted the urge to kick him under the table. "Notorious gangster?" asked Angelica, wrinkling her pert little nose. "You're so silly, Tink. How do you and Gan-Gan know each other?"

She linked her arm through his and pressed her cheek against his shoulder. It seemed sweet, but I knew Angelica well enough to understand that it was the equivalent of a dog marking its territory.

"We met on the plane here. He recognized me from an old article in *Elf* magazine about my family. And from the article in the paper about Jax and I cracking the candico-cane case. How funny is that?" I knew it bothered Angelica that I came from a famous family. I also knew she hated it if anyone else got attention. I shouldn't have enjoyed the flash of irritation I saw in her eyes, but I did. Also, I was two watermelon daiquiris in, and rum made me feisty. "How did the two of you end up together? I'm sure it was super romantic."

She smiled. "It was, actually. I'd been helping at a home for orphaned elflings, and the director said one of their most generous sponsors had stopped by to drop off even more donations. I asked to meet him to thank him. That was Gan-Gan, and the rest is history." She let out an excited squeak. "Wait. You should volunteer there with me, Tink. I'm sure you have lots of time, and the kids would relate to you since your parents are dead, too."

I felt Jax stiffen next to me. I put a hand on his thigh. For some reason, the way she said it felt like an insult, but before I could respond, Ganja stepped in. "I was orphaned at a young age, too, Angelica, but the desire to help has to be a calling. Something in your heart. You can't force someone to do it, and Tink doesn't owe anyone anything. That's not what true charity is about."

His words surprised me. "You lost your parents, too?"

He nodded, his expression haunted. "I was seven."

"Like me."

"Like you," he said, giving me a sad half-smile.

Angelica did not appreciate our moment of solidarity. "And I was adopted. I never knew my birth parents, but we all have our burdens to bear. You had your grandmother and your uncle, Tink. It's a little different. Ganja had no one. He grew up on the streets."

Ganja squeezed her hand. "Enough about me and sad things from the past. Let's leave those things behind, and let's leave behind our professions as well. Tonight, we aren't EBI agents, gangsters, or beauty queens. We are strangers who met on vacation. These two are here to celebrate, Angelica, and so are we."

"Agreed," said Jax, putting an arm around my shoulders as he called the waiter over. "This calls for champagne."

Even though I'd already had way too much champagne today, Jax's suggestion was a good one. We toasted each other and sipped the champagne as we chatted and enjoyed a fantastic meal. Angelica seemed to make an effort to play nice. Maybe Ganja was right when he'd told me people change on the plane. Maybe Angelica wasn't a total shrew anymore.

For a second, I considered texting Noelle to let her know what was happening, but I remembered Noelle wasn't speaking to me, and it made me sad. She would have enjoyed hearing that Miss Perfect Everything, Angelica Frost, was now dating a notorious gangster. That level of gossip felt even more delicious than my fake marriage to Jax.

Angelica got up to go to the restroom. She seemed to be gone for quite a long time, but girls like Angelica usually needed to reapply lipstick and makeup and do their hair or whatever when they went to the restroom. They took the term "powder my nose" literally. She came back with flawless makeup and hair perfectly in place, and I caught her eyeing my ring as we waited for the dessert menu. She seemed extremely interested in my diamond.

"Isn't it incredible?" I asked.

"It is," she said, taking my hand in hers so she could study it more closely, a puzzled frown on her pretty face. "Strange, because it looks like a rochtar diamond. I can tell because of the little flames hidden inside it."

"You're right. It is a rochtar diamond." I tilted my hand back and forth in light from the tiki torches surrounding the patio. I'd never been keen on diamonds or jewelry, but this piece mesmerized me. "Why is that strange?"

"Because all rochtar diamonds are the property of..." Her voice trailed off. She gazed at Jax with new interest. "Oh. I see."

I had no idea what she meant, but before I could ask, several servers appeared. One carried a beautiful cake covered in flowers. They sang a song to us congratulating Jax and me on our nuptials and wishing us many elflings and nothing but happiness in the future.

"Thank you," I said, and everyone in the restaurant clapped as soon as they finished singing. "That's so kind."

The head waiter cut the cake, giving both Jax and me a generous slice. Ganja and Angelica had a different dessert with lots of fruit and cream. When I offered them some of our cake, Ganja demurred.

"No. Enjoy it. That cake is for you."

The waiter agreed. "Yes. It's our special honeymoon treat. I'll pack the rest for you to take back to your room." He grinned, a twinkle in his dark eyes. "And may your lives be as sweet and surprising as this cake."

He put the remaining cake in a box and tied it with a bow. After he left, Jax lifted his fork, indicating the cake. "Shall we?" he asked. He knew how I felt about sweets.

"Yes, please."

I dug in, delighted. I loved cake, but this was the most delicious cake I'd ever tasted. To my surprise, Jax seemed to be enjoying his slice as well.

"Oh, my," he said. "I don't usually eat cake, but this is incredible."

"You have no idea," said Ganja under his breath, but I heard him and looked at him curiously.

"What do you mean?" I asked.

He waved a hand. "Never mind. Enjoy your cake. It's a nature elf honeymoon tradition."

I sighed happily. "I love nature elf honeymoon traditions." I glanced up at Jax, suddenly unable to stop myself from blurting out the words on my tongue. "And I love being here with you. Even when things are a total mess and I shouldn't be happy, you make me crazy happy, Jax."

Had I said that out loud? I nearly freaked out, but Jax must have thought I was putting on an act for Ganja and Angelica. He smiled at me in a loopy way and took my hand in his.

"It defies logic, but you make me crazy happy, too."

To my surprise, he leaned forward and kissed me on the lips. It was not a chaste kiss. It was pretty freaking hot. His delicious mouth pressed against mine, tasting like cake and sin.

I must have had more to drink than I'd realized because I grabbed hold of his shirt and brought him closer. I would have climbed on his lap, but Ganja cleared his throat, reminding us we had spectators.

"Sorry," I said, but I kept my body pressed against Jax's. I needed to be close to him, and he seemed to feel the same. He nuzzled my neck with a growl. It took everything inside not to throw him down on the restaurant floor and have my way with him.

I exhaled slowly, trying to control myself. I thought eating more cake might sober me up, but it seemed to make things worse rather than better. I was in deep doo-doo.

"Wow," I said as Jax continued to nuzzle my neck. "Those daiquiris must have been stronger than I realized."

Ganja winked at Angelica. "Yes, the daiquiris were something."

I put a hand on my head. The restaurant had started spinning. "I'm seriously sloshed. Blotto. Trashed. Drunk as a skunk. Holy moly. What's going on?"

And Jax, giggling as he kissed his way up my neck, was no help at all. "Drunk as a skunk," he said. "Druuuunk as a skuuuunk."

Ganja called the waiter over. "I think it's time for the love birds to return to their nest."

Jax nodded. "Great idea. Come on, wifey." He stood, swaying slightly on his feet, and held out his hand to me. I took it, feeling unsteady myself.

Ganja and Angelica got up as well. They were not

unsteady. They seemed perfectly fine, even though we'd had the same amount to drink.

I assumed we were both emotionally and physically exhausted. That was why we'd been affected more by the alcohol.

"Will the two of you be okay?" asked Ganja. "Do you need help?"

"Definitely not," said Jax, pulling me close and kissing the top of my head. "We've got this."

I gave Ganja a thumbs up and an exaggerated wink as we headed down the jungle path toward the honeymoon suite. That seemed to be my standard farewell when dealing with Ganja. I waved and shouted over my shoulder, "We've got this."

At least I meant to say, "We've got this." It came out more like, "Weeeeeve shot piss," which made Jax and me laugh so hard we could barely walk.

"Did I say, 'We've shot piss' to notorious gangster Ganja Green and my high school arch-nemesis Angelica?"

"You did, and it was hilarious. You are hilarious."

Jax paused to stare down at me with a huge grin. He was always so serious. When he smiled at me like this, it felt like a gift. I reached up to touch his face.

"And you are beautiful. I love it when you smile like that, Jaxy."

He groaned and looped an arm around my shoulders as we continued to the honeymoon suite. "I thought I told you not to call me that."

"I can't help it. It's my special name for you. Like how Angelica uses Gan-Gan for Ganja. It's sweet."

This time we both laughed so hard we had to stop walking. Every time we took a step, I'd say, "Gan-Gan," and it would start again. It took a while, but we finally made it back to our tree. I wrapped my arms around Jax's waist and leaned on him heavily as I stared at the honeymoon suite. It seemed very high up at the moment. I wondered how we'd make it there without breaking our necks when a hotel employee appeared out of nowhere and offered to hoist us up. He realized we were incapable of hoisting ourselves at the moment.

"You are a lifesaver," I said. "Literally."

He laughed as he instructed Jax to go first, a good call. I worried I might fall if I went up there alone. After Jax was safely waiting on the balcony for me, it was my turn to be hoisted.

I gazed at Jax as I sat on the swing. The wind was a whisper in the trees, and behind him, the sky was inky black and filled with stars, but all I could think about was him. All I could look at was his face.

I saw so much there. Longing. Desire. Loneliness. Pain. And something else too.

Could it be hope? Or was it hunger?

I leaned back in the swing, unable to take my eyes off him. When I reached the top, and he pulled me onto the safety of the balcony, I still couldn't break my gaze away from his face. He was the perfect mix of dark and light, familiar and mysterious, and I wanted him so badly I ached with it. I poured all that emotion into a single word.

"Jax."

He cupped my face in his big hands and pressed his forehead to mine. "What is it, Tink?"

I couldn't answer. Well, not in words. Instead, I wrapped my arms around his neck and kissed him with all the pent-up desire I'd held inside since the first moment we met. I'd forced myself to stay away so long. I couldn't do it any longer. And Jax seemed to feel the same way.

"Oh, Tink," he said, murmuring the words against my mouth. "I know I shouldn't want you like this. I know I should fight against it, but I can't. I meant what I said in the restaurant. You make me happy. You're impulsive and have no respect for authority, and you might be a bit mad as well, but it doesn't matter because I'm hopelessly, madly into you."

"Jax. I'm into you too." I paused. "Wait. Did you say I was nuts?"

He kissed me deeply. "In only the best possible ways."

"Uh, okay." His words should have pissed me off, but he started doing something to my ear with his tongue that made me forget to be angry. "Well, you aren't nuts. You're good, honorable, kind, and so smart that it intimidated me sometimes, but I wouldn't have it any other way."

"You like me for my intellect?" he asked as he pushed aside the straps of my sundress and kissed his way down between the valley of my breasts.

"Yes, but you're hot, too. Like smoking hot. That's not a bad thing, either. Also..."

I wanted to say more. I tried to tell him how he'd changed everything for me, and I wanted to be a better person because of him. So that I could deserve him. Instead, a strange feeling came over me.

"Uh-oh."

He eyed me curiously. "Uh-oh?"

My stomach heaved. I stared at his face, horrified but unable to contain it any longer. "I think I'm going to be sick."

THIRTEEN

After a visit to the emergency room, during which we discovered I'd had a terrible reaction to whatever aphrodisiac those well-intentioned nature elves had put in our special cake, Jax and I returned to our room battered and puffy.

Well, I was battered and puffy. Jax was perfect.

We fell asleep, fully clothed and exhausted. The following day, I woke up moaning. Jax moaned, too, and I reached over to pat him. We'd slept side by side on the enormous honeymoon bed. I'd gotten sick several times on the way to the ER and smelled faintly of vomit and bad choices. Jax had taken care of me. I think he may have gotten sick at some point as well, but that part seemed a little fuzzy.

"What happened?" I asked. "Was it the cake, or did we get food poisoning?"

I opened my eyes a crack to look at him. He appeared even paler than usual.

"Both. Someone accidentally doubled the dose of aphrodisiac in the honeymoon cake. I spoke with the doctor. They're waiting for a toxicology report, but apparently, someone also accidentally put a mildly toxic flower on the cake as a decoration."

"That's a lot of accidents for one cake. Why didn't you get sick, too?"

"You ate the flowers. I only ate the cake."

"I see." Once again, my love of sweets and pretty things had led to trouble. "They were delicious, though."

Jax nodded. "Agreed. They always make that cake, but no one has ever reacted this way. Maybe because they've never unintentionally doubled the dose of aphrodisiac before."

I wrinkled my nose. "Lucky me."

"Indeed. We're lucky you didn't eat more. You could have died. They said someone had mismarked the bottle. They sent their deepest apologies, and they're covering the cost of our stay." He sat up and turned, putting his feet on the floor. "Which they should."

I had to agree with him. "Freaking honeymoon cake. It was good, though. I mean, for something toxic."

He ran a hand over his head. "Do you mind if I use the bathroom? I want to wash my face."

I waved a hand at him. "Go ahead. It's going to take me some time to get vertical again."

He headed to the bathroom, and I heard him splashing his face with water and brushing his teeth. I stared at the white canopy of our honeymoon bed, remembering what had happened before I got sick and mortified by how I behaved.

Had I seriously told Jax he made me crazy happy? I frowned, recalling even more of the evening, and sat up so quickly my head spun.

Had Jax said I made him crazy happy, too?

He had. I was sure of it. And he said a bunch of other

nice things as well. The question was, how would he play it this morning? Would he want to talk about it or pretend it never happened?

I got my answer rather quickly. He came out of the bathroom with a scowl and glanced at his watch. "We have to be at the meditation center in an hour. Are you well enough to go, or would you prefer I went on my own?"

"I've got this," I said, lifting a finger. "I'm coming."

"Fine, but you'll need to shower, eat, and get ready as quickly as possible. No dawdling."

I pushed aside the sheets and got out of bed. "Aye, aye, captain."

I couldn't keep the snark out of my tone. His reaction stung. Not that I expected him to swear his undying love to me, but it hurt that he didn't even plan on addressing the elephant in the room.

The superb hotel employees who'd nearly killed me the night before had thoughtfully hoisted up a sumptuous breakfast for us. It sat on a tray on the swing, and despite what had happened, it looked very appealing. Jax put it on a small wooden table on the balcony and sat on one of the two comfy chairs. I grabbed a triangle of dry toast and munched it as I stared at the misty morning jungle and the Mayan temple in the distance. It was terrific, but Jax was right. We needed to get moving.

"Do you mind if I shower?"

He let out a grunt that I interpreted as an affirmative response. Although I wanted to sit down and discuss things, we didn't have time. We had a job to do.

The shower was huge and had all the accouterments of a world-class spa. I washed my hair with a shampoo that smelled like sweet tropical flowers and scrubbed my body with a soap that made my skin feel soft and satiny.

Being in the shower gave me time to think. I needed that time.

I meant it when I told Jax he made me happy last night. It felt strange to admit that, even to myself, but I knew it was true.

The big question was, could he have meant it, too?

I shook my head, not wanting to go there. Even if he did care for me, it changed nothing. He was still my boss—sort of. And he was still a dark elf. As much as he seemed to like the North Pole, he would get sick of it eventually. Everyone did. And where would we be if that happened? I wouldn't last long in the world of the dark elves. They'd eat me alive. The fact that Jax liked being around me made him the exception to the other elves in his tribe.

Dark elves did not like Christmas elves. They thought we were shallow and stupid, and they were kind of right. But I wasn't as shallow or silly as the average Christmas elf, which may have been why Jax liked me.

But could he like me? For real?

I covered my face with my hands. It seemed impossible. I'd screwed up everything. I screwed up my life, and I screwed up the case, and I even screwed up our fake honeymoon. There was no way he could love me. Even if a little part of my heart hoped that could be the case, I'd been burned by those dreams before. I wouldn't let it happen again.

I needed to focus on the task at hand. Scarlet was dead. We needed to find her killer, and we also needed to stop whoever was sending the rock candy to the North Pole. And we didn't have much time to do it. Jax and I may or may not have jobs when we get back. We had to make the most of each minute, and I needed to tell him what I knew.

I turned off the shower and dried my hair and body

with white, fluffy towels. I brushed my hair, put it into a bun, and covered myself in body lotion. After I smoothed it in, I put on a plush robe and rejoined Jax on the balcony. He was sipping a cup of coffee and looked marginally better than when he'd first woken up.

"We have coffee," he said. "And monkeys."

He pointed up to a nearby tree. Several large, black monkeys were perched there, staring at us. I let out a surprised laugh.

"What kind of monkeys are those?"

One opened its mouth and let out a loud howl. The other two followed, creating quite the racket.

"Howler monkeys," he said, draining the last of his coffee. "But I guess that's obvious. I'm going to take my shower now."

I gave him a thumbs up, my eyes still on the screaming monkeys. "Go for it."

While Jax showered, I dressed in a long, light, comfortable dress and went out to eat breakfast. I took some photos of the monkeys for Grandma Gingersnap. She responded with, *Do not touch the monkeys. They carry diseases. That's the last thing you need right now.*

I could almost hear her irritation in her text. I responded. *And thanks for telling Jax where I went. Traitor.*

She answered immediately. Her reply was not what I expected.

I had no choice. You needed him. 8==D.

I stared at the text. Grandma. *What was that? Did you send me a penis?*

Bubbles appeared, and I waited for her to type out the next message. *No, Tink. You have such a dirty mind. That's a smiley face. Be good. Please. For once.*

I responded with her version of a smiley face. *Got it, and you're right. I do need him.* 8==D.

I'd let her interpret that how she'd like. I decided not to tell her about the emergency room visit or the aphrodisiac. That would involve a phone call, not just a text, and I had no time for that this morning.

I took a long sip of coffee. This was paradise with lush trees, beautiful flowers, exotic birds, and monkeys. I was about to offer my muffin to one of those monkeys when I noticed a small note on the tray.

Do not feed the monkeys, especially Felix. He is not hungry. He is only acting. Also, he likes to make rude gestures and throw poo at people. Watch out.

I laughed and sent the monkeys an apologetic look. "Sorry, guys. I guess the food is all mine."

They responded by screaming at me. I had to guess the biggest one was Felix. He grabbed his private parts and displayed them in a rather aggressive way. I think he started to masturbate, but I couldn't be sure. Jax came out in the middle of it.

"Well, it looks like things are again going according to plan," he said.

"They didn't throw poo at us," I said. "Silver linings."

At that moment, Felix wound up his arm like a major league pitcher and threw poo at us. It landed on the balcony right next to me with a plop.

"I spoke too soon," I said. "I was done eating anyway, Felix. So there."

I got up and gave him the finger. Not my proudest moment. To my surprise, Felix gave me the finger in response. He grabbed his balls before climbing higher in the tree and heading into the forest.

I gaped at Jax. "Did you see that?"

Jax's lips twitched in response. "I did. Can we please leave if you're done making friends with the local wildlife?"

"Lead the way," I said but kept my eyes on the trees. Felix had drawn a line in the sand. I had a feeling that monkey would be back, and I wanted to be ready for it.

FOURTEEN

Howler monkeys didn't attack us on our way to the meditation center. We did run into several apologetic and completely naked hotel employees and also into Angelica and Ganja. They had clothing on—a good thing. And apparently, the news had spread that I'd ended up in the emergency room. To my surprise, Angelica displayed a bit of kindness and concern—a new look for her.

"You poor thing. What a way to spend your honeymoon. Are you okay?"

"I'm fine. I mean, it's not the first time I've had my stomach pumped, and I'm sure it won't be the last."

Ganja smothered a laugh. He did that a lot around me. Angelica shushed him and linked my arm in hers as we walked down the winding jungle path together. She had a yoga mat strapped to her back, and Ganja and Jax followed a few feet behind us.

"We're not doing yoga, are we?" I asked, eyeing her pretty, pink mat. It matched her pretty, pink leggings and her teeny, tiny top. She even had a coordinating pink ribbon in her hair. I did not have ribbons in my hair, and if I had to do yoga, I'd puke up my breakfast. True story. It had happened before.

"No. I'm attending a private jungle yoga session this morning. I'll be alone in the rainforest with monkeys and everything. They have additional slots available later if you want to sign up."

"Uh, no. I met some monkeys this morning. Not a fan."

I assumed Felix was back when I heard a rustle above us in the trees. I jumped in front of Angelica and immediately put my hands up, ready to defend myself with my karate skills.

Note to self: I had no karate skills.

"Are you okay?" asked Angelica.

"I'm fine," I said, expecting to see Felix, the testicle-grabbing, poop-throwing howler monkey pop out of the foliage at any moment. "Stand back, Angelica. I've got this."

A beautifully colored bird emerged from the trees and took off into the sky. I let out a breath and relaxed. Angelica stared at me oddly.

"You're acting weirder than usual."

"I'm not acting," I said with a tight smile. Knowing I had to play nice, I again linked my arm through hers. "Sorry. It's been a long week."

She patted my hand where it rested on her forearm. "I bet." She snuck a glance over her shoulder. Ganja and Jax were deep in conversation and ignored us. "Can we talk?"

"Sure."

I had no idea where this might lead, but Angelica gazed at me intently, a flush creeping into her cheeks. Even her pointed little ears turned pink. She had something on her mind.

"I wanted to say I'm happy for you. Jax seems like a great guy, and he's totally in love with you. Also, knowing who he is, I have to admit, I'm impressed. Your family is North Pole royalty, but Jax is next level."

I had no idea what she meant but figured it was easiest to nod in agreement. "He is."

I gave her a thumbs up with the hand that wasn't currently locked on her elbow and winked—my new nervous tic. I couldn't stop myself. The harder I tried, the more often it happened. It took everything in me not to do it a second time.

Angelica didn't seem to notice. "But there is something else as well." She paused, biting her lower lip. "I wanted to apologize for how I treated you when we were younger."

"What do you mean?" I asked because I could think of a thousand ways she'd hurt my feelings growing up.

"Like when I called you Stinky Tinky in elementary school."

"Ahhh. The old Stinky Tinky barb. I remember it well."

"And when you developed before everyone else in middle school, I made fun of you in the locker room after gym class."

I cringed as bad memories washed over me like suds in that communal shower. "My boobs have always been both a blessing and a curse, but you weren't the only one who—"

"And in high school, I started that rumor that you'd slept with the whole sledding team. Boys and girls. And the coaches. And the mascot, Simpy the Seal."

I narrowed my eyes at her. "That was you?"

"Yes."

"I guess I have you to thank for the Skanky Tinky nickname, too."

"You do. I'm so sorry."

I sighed, recalling exactly how much it had hurt to be called those names and the shame I'd felt over the whole sledding team thing. And Simpy had been an actual seal. I couldn't even figure out the mechanics of that one, but I'd always assumed it was Frank Yummy who'd started the rumor. It seemed like something he would have done. Even in high school, he'd been a bit of a pervert.

But Frank was dead now, and Angelica and I were both adults. It was time to move on.

"All of that happened years ago, Angelica. The statute of limitations is up. There is nothing to forgive."

"Really?"

"Yes. Really. But I don't understand why you hated me so much."

"I didn't hate you," she said in a soft, sad voice. "I was jealous of you."

I tripped on a vine on the jungle floor. If Angelica hadn't been holding onto me, I would have fallen.

"You were jealous of me? But you were the prettiest and most popular elf in our class. I was a weirdo who may or may not have had intimate relations with a harbor seal."

She laughed, nudging me. "You were not a weirdo. I saw you as my competition. You're whip smart and beautiful, but it's more than your looks and brains. I may have been popular, but I didn't have a best friend as loyal as Noelle or a boyfriend as perfect as Win."

Her words stabbed me since Noelle wasn't speaking to me at the moment and Win and I were ancient history, but I nodded anyway. "Yeah, I was lucky with those two."

"Yes, but it was more than that. My adoptive parents were good people, but my dad worked on the toy car assembly line, and my mom was a teacher. We never came close to the illustrious Holly family. Not for wealth. Not for status. Not for anything. There was no competing with you, so I did the only thing I could. I tried to make you feel small, so I'd feel better about myself, but it didn't work. The more I did it, the worse I felt."

"You were a kid. We all did stuff like that when we were younger, things we aren't proud of doing. Heck, I've even done stuff like that as an adult."

It wasn't a lie, and Angelica gave me a grateful smile. "Thanks for understanding. I wish I could go back and change things, but I can't. Maybe we can move on from here? I'd like to be your friend, Tink. It's what I've always wanted."

I swallowed hard. "I'd like that. I could use a friend right now."

"You could?" she asked, her brows furrowed.

"Yes. And I think you'd be perfect for the job."

We'd reached the retreat center, and Jax and Ganja caught up. Angelica surprised me with a hug. "Thank you, Tink."

I hugged her back. "No. Thank you."

Angelica left for her jungle yoga. Ganja waved and began heading down a different path, but I stopped him.

"Wait. Aren't you doing meditation?"

He shook his head. "No. It's for couples. We planned on doing it, but Angelica was more interested in yoga. I'm having a massage instead. Shall we get together for drinks tonight before dinner?"

"Sure," I said, giving Jax a pointed look. We'd only signed up for this class because Ganja was on the roster.

A gong sounded, announcing the start of class, and Ganja eyed us curiously. "Aren't you going in?"

"Oh. Yes. Of course. A massage sounds nice, though."

"They were booked solid for this morning. I can put you on the schedule while I'm there if you'd like," he said. "They might have something available for later today."

"Okay."

There was another awkward pause. Jax took my arm. "We'd better go in," he said, tilting his head to indicate the meditation center. He was right. We had no other option.

"Fudgity fudge cakes," I said under my breath.

"My sentiments exactly," said Jax. "But we don't want to make Ganja suspicious."

"You're right. At least I got things ironed out with Angelica. It'll make it easier for us to spend time with them. I feel like we made some progress."

I sighed as I climbed the wooden steps to the meditation center. Even if things hadn't exactly gone according to plan, I hoped we were heading in the right direction.

That feeling lasted until we entered the retreat center and saw our instructor. I grabbed Jax's arm. "Oh, no. It's the Forest Wench."

Many years ago, when I'd stupidly taken a job in collections on the North Pole, the first customer I'd dealt with had been a nature elf named Lily Garland. I'd been in the position for ten minutes, and Lily scammed me into believing she was a poor, old, down-on-her-luck widow who'd bought a toy for her grandson and couldn't pay for it because her house burned down. And she'd lost her job. And she was sick. And her dog ran away.

Jax knew the whole story. Everyone in collections knew the story, too. His eyes widened in surprise.

"You're kidding, right?"

"Sadly, I am not."

I should have known better than to trust someone like Lily Garland, but it was my first day on the job. I'd ended up using my credit card to pay for the toy. Lily had thanked me profusely and stole my credit card info and my identity.

I got fired immediately, which was for the best, but it took me years to repair my credit rating.

Much later, I'd found out Lily wasn't an old grandmother with a dead dog. She was only a few years older than me and had a better credit score than me as well.

"These things only happen to you," said Jax, shaking his head in disbelief. As he went to sign us in for the class, I stood by the door, staring daggers at Lily. When she saw me, her face lit up like greeting an old friend.

"Tinklebelle Holly. We meet at last." She took my hand and stared at me with tears glistening in her pretty, purple eyes. She also had pretty purple hair and wore a dress the same color accentuating her slim body. She pulled me off to the side of the room. "I've wanted to speak with you for years. I was elated when I saw you on my class roster for this morning. I'm so grateful the universe has finally seen fit to bring us together at last."

"Oh, I've wanted to speak with you, too, Lily. Trust me."

Before I could continue, she handed me a fat envelope with my name on it. I stared down at it in confusion.

"It's what I owe you," she said, her expression sincere and her hand still holding mine. "Plus interest."

"But you got away with it. Why are you paying me back now?"

"I was in a bad place all those years ago. I'd gotten trapped in an abusive relationship, had started using drugs, and my prospects were bleak. My choices hovered between prostitution and suicide. Suicide seemed the better option, but I found out I was pregnant." She swallowed hard. "And that was the day I got the call from you that changed my life."

"Because I was a sucker, and you were able to scam me?"

"No, because you showed me kindness when I needed it most," she said, her tone gentle. "I used your credit card to get an apartment and enroll in classes. You saved my life, Tink, and I'll be forever grateful to you." She pulled up a photo on her phone of an adorable little elf with pigtails and purple eyes like Lily. "This is my daughter. I named her after you. Tinklebelle Holly Garland. We call her Holly."

"Holly Garland? Wow," I said, swallowing hard. If Lily was attempting to scam me again, she'd gone the extra mile by producing a kid who looked like her mini-me. I handed her back the envelope. "Use this for your little girl. And thank you for explaining. I always wondered why you did it, and now I know. Also, I kind of owe you one. I wasn't cut out for collections."

"Obviously, you were not," she said with a shy smile.

"Obviously." I returned her smile with one of my own. "But I'm glad I helped, even if I didn't do it on purpose."

She placed the envelope on a table and took my hands in hers. "Call it fate or karma, but something brought us together all those years ago and brought us together again today. There was a reason for it, and there is a reason for it now, and I'm grateful for it. Maybe it's my turn to help you." She glanced around the room as the other guests took their places, before turning back to me. "Let's begin."

FIFTEEN

"What happened?" asked Jax when I joined him on the tatami mat floor in the center of the meditation room. It had large, open windows on all four walls, and a breeze flowed in, caressing our skin. It felt heavenly in the jungle heat. As a North Pole elf, I was used to cooler climes.

"Long story," I said, keeping my voice low as I sat cross-legged next to him.

He rolled his eyes. "It's always a long story," he said as Lily rang a gong.

"Before we get started," she said, lighting something that looked like a small bundle of tree bark tied together with string and sitting in a bowl. "I'd like to acknowledge a special guest. Tinklebelle Holly." She folded her hands in prayer and gave me a low bow. "Many years ago, Tink saved my life through a single act of random kindness to a total stranger. I'd like to dedicate this class to her and random acts of kindness."

Jax lifted an eyebrow at me. "Wow."

"Exactly."

Lily went to the front of the room and took off her dress.

Half of the other attendees disrobed as well. The smell of whatever she'd lit wafted over me, making me feel dizzy. I looked at Jax, wondering if we should take off our clothing, too, and he gave me a subtle shake of his head.

"No way," he said under his breath.

I held back a laugh. I loved making Jax uncomfortable. I was tempted to take off my clothing for the heck of it but held myself back.

Lily rang the gong again. "Let us begin."

She looked gorgeous naked. I did not. I was kind of glad I'd kept my clothing on.

Meditation was not at all what I expected. I figured it would be torture for an elf like me since I had the attention span of a gnat. Surprisingly, with Lily's soothing voice gently instructing us on what to do and the sweet breeze scented with jungle flowers wafting in from the open windows, I found it wasn't hard to get into it. The smell of the burning bark helped, too. It seemed to relax me almost as much as the meditation.

After taking some long, deep breaths, Lily led us through each part of our body, making us relax our feet, legs, arms, and faces. Every time my attention would wander, she'd bring my focus back to this room. Back to the meditation. I felt extremely calm and chill by the end, but it didn't stop there.

"And now for the couples' portion of the meditation," she said. "Turn and face your partner. Move closer, so that your knees are touching. Reach out and hold your partner's hands."

My head swam, but we did as she instructed. Jax held both of my hands in his larger ones and stared deeply into my eyes. For a moment, I forgot we were only at this retreat to spy on Ganja and get information from him. It felt like Jax and I were the only two elves in the world.

"Breath as one. In and out. Feel the circle of energy coursing through you, from one body to the next. Feel your partner's warmth. Their thoughts. Their pain. Their love. Feel all of them, past and present, and allow them to feel all of you."

As the smoke swirled around us, a weird tingling sensation overcame me. I stared deeply into Jax's fathomless eyes, and we breathed together, silent and still. I'd never felt so connected to anyone in my life. I didn't precisely see or understand his past or his pain, but I felt it, almost like it was my own.

"Now take this opportunity, this moment in time, to share how you feel about them."

She may have meant to say something affirming, but I chose a different method, and she didn't have to ask me twice. There wasn't much distance between Jax and me to begin with, but I closed it in order to kiss him, pouring all of my pent-up emotions and frustrations and desire into that single act. He responded with a groan, and that noise he made, deep in his throat, was the final straw.

I wasn't sure how it happened, but I ended up climbing on top of Jax, straddling him, and wrapping my legs around his waist as I kissed him passionately. He tangled his fingers in my hair. I cupped his face in my hands. We both forgot we were in a room with other people for a moment. I blamed it on all the excellent meditation endorphins. It wasn't until Lily rang the gong again that we returned to reality.

Jax gazed at me, aroused and a little befuddled. I loved it when he looked at me that way. I wanted to tear off his black t-shirt and have my way with him, but I suddenly remembered we weren't alone, and the entire class stared at us, dumbfounded.

"Oops. Sorry," I said as I climbed off Jax's lap.

No one else had made out with their partner during this exercise. Jax and I were the anomalies.

One of the elves let out a giggle. "You go, girl," she said.

Lily approached us and placed a hand on each of our heads. "Honeymooners," she said, giving us a warm smile. "Your love is a beautiful thing. It shines from both of you like a glorious beacon. Thank you for sharing it with us. Thank you for allowing us to witness the passion you feel for each other." She lowered her voice, a twinkle in her eyes. "And get a room, you two. Seriously. I'm glad you kept your clothing on at the start of class. Otherwise, we may have seen more than a few kisses."

The rest of the class laughed, clapping in agreement. A few yelled out catcalls.

"Kiss her again," said one older water elf in the corner. She had flowing white hair with rainbow highlights. She clapped her hands, saying, "Kiss her, kiss her," over and over again.

Soon the rest of the room chanted and clapped along with her. "Kiss her. Kiss her. Kiss her."

Jax's pale face flushed with embarrassment, but he got to his feet and pulled me up, holding me close against his body. I felt his desire pressing against me and saw the raw hunger in his eyes. If he was putting on a show, Jax was a better actor than I realized.

"May I?" he asked, soft enough that only I could hear him.

"You'd better," I said, wrapping my arms around his neck. "We don't want to disappoint our audience."

This time when Jax kissed me, I sensed the battle

within him. He wanted me, possibly as much as I wanted him, but there were other elements at play here, and we both knew it.

He was technically my boss and too honorable to ignore that fact.

We were here to work, and lives were at stake.

He still felt angry with me for what had happened in Scarlet's club.

He didn't trust me.

Not completely.

I'd never lied to him about my feelings for him, but I had lied to him about other things. And trust, once broken, was hard to earn back.

I sensed it the moment Jax made his decision. It was apparent, mostly because he broke off the kiss, lifted me into his arms, and flung me over his shoulder like a cave elf.

"Thank you, Lily," he said, patting my butt. "And you're right. Time for wifey and I to get a room."

The guests cheered, and now I was the one blushing. Today had already taken so many surprising turns. Making up with Angelica had been a big one. I had no idea what might happen next, but it bothered me that I'd spent years of my life despising her. I wondered what else I'd been wasting time on. One of those things was probably fighting the attraction I felt for Jax.

As he carried me toward the honeymoon suite, I decided that was one thing I could fix. And I intended to do it immediately.

Jax and I made it to the tree. We climbed up the winding staircase, stopping periodically to kiss along the way. He couldn't seem to stop touching me, caressing me. I felt the same way. And although I didn't think I could want him more, my desire for him grew with each step we took.

By the time we reached the balcony, I was panting, and not from exertion. So was Jax.

"This might be a huge mistake," he said, kissing me as he pressed me against the outside wall of the treehouse. "But I find I don't care anymore."

"Agreed," I said. "Take me to bed. Now."

We stumbled into the bedroom, and that's when we realized we weren't alone. Felix, the howler monkey, and his friends were inside. They'd torn it apart and seemed to be having a monkey orgy. Felix was making love to a female monkey right on our bed. We made it in time to watch him climax.

"Ew," I said, coming out of whatever fog I'd been under. Lily had been burning more than incense. What was it with these nature elves drugging us without our consent? It was getting out of hand, but I had monkeys to deal with right now.

Felix locked eyes with me, and I swear he cackled. He squatted and pooped on my pillow before running out the open door with his friends.

"Crap," said Jax, appropriately enough, as he shut the door behind Felix. "I'd better call housekeeping."

As Jax made the phone call, I realized several things at once.

First of all, Jax and I were not meant to be together. Not in a sexual way, at least. It seemed like the whole universe conspired to keep us apart, and we should listen.

Secondly, we'd locked the door before we'd left for the meditation center, but it had been open when we returned. We hadn't noticed because we were thinking about other things (meaning the horizontal mambo).

Thirdly, something else was wrong. Our suitcases had

been tossed aside, and our belongings were thrown all over the floor.

"Freaking monkeys," said Jax, staring around at the chaos with his hands on his hips.

"I hope it was the monkeys," I said, panic settling in my chest. "Because if it wasn't them, who was it?"

"And what were they looking for?" Jax paused, his eyes scanning the room. "Is anything missing?"

"It's hard to tell." I rubbed my temples. "Oh, gosh. I feel so strange. I think I'm high."

"I think we're both high, but let's focus. Why would someone ransack our room?"

"I don't know. Maybe we're jumping to conclusions. Maybe we left a door or window open and didn't realize it. Maybe Felix ransacked it."

"Felix?"

"The monkey that was having sex on our bed. He and his friends might be responsible for this mess."

"Or maybe not." Jax inspected the room. He crouched down and studied a spot on the floor by the door. I joined him.

"A footprint?" It looked like the tread of a tennis shoe.

Jax pulled out a piece of paper and began tracing the print. "Yes, and unless Felix wears shoes that are a men's size eight or a women's size ten, someone else was in our room. You wear a nine. I wear an eleven. Neither of us made that footprint. If it wasn't us, who was it?"

My heart sank. He was right. "I don't know."

"Neither do I, and that's what we need to figure out."

SIXTEEN

The resort staff arrived quickly. It was a team that included the manager, a cleaning crew, and a game warden. They were all apologetic and shocked by what had happened. Apparently, Felix had never done anything like this before.

"I mean, he's stolen food and a few odds and ends," said Reggie, the game warden. "But never something like this. I blame the cake."

Felix had found the one remaining slice of our extra special honeymoon cake. We'd left it in our fridge and forgotten about it.

"Well, that does explain the monkey orgy," I said. "Not something I care to witness ever again.

"Felix is fairly predictable," said Reggie, jotting something in a small notebook. "He likes to stash his loot in one particular tree. If he stole something from you, I can see if it's there. Are you missing anything important?"

Jax shook his head. "Not that we know of, but it's hard to tell."

"Okay." Reggie put his notebook into the right breast pocket of his khaki-colored shirt. "If the monkeys have something of yours, I'll do my best to get it back to you. I promise."

With a nod, he set off. The hotel manager, Cress Crispin, looked around at the mess of a room with a pained expression on his face.

"While our staff is at work and Reggie is searching for Felix, we'd like to offer you a relaxing afternoon at the spa. Our treat. It will allow us to apologize again and for our housekeeping team to tidy this up."

Jax and I stared around the room. It would require more than tidying.

"Tink can go to the spa," said Jax. "I know Ganja Green had a massage earlier. I might hang out with him."

Cress pulled out his phone. "I can't say for certain, but normally after a massage, our guests like to enjoy a soak in the mineral springs. Mr. Green should be there soon. You can join him. And for you, Ms. Holly, I've arranged a full body spa treatment. It seems like you need it after this." He put his phone back into his pocket and shook his head. "Please enjoy it and accept our apologies once more for this inconvenience. First, the disaster with the honeymoon cake, and now this. We've never had anything like this ever happen before."

"That's because Tink Holly has never been a guest here before," said Jax.

Cress laughed politely at what he assumed was a joke, but I knew Jax wasn't joking. As Jax went into the bathroom to change into his swim trunks, Cress opened the door to the balcony with a bow.

"Shall we?"

I looked over my shoulder at the closed bathroom door. I wanted to tell Jax about the flash drive, but every time I tried, I either got distracted, or disaster struck. The longer I waited, the more it seemed like I was hiding it from him, but I had no choice at the moment, so I followed Cress out the door.

The spa was beautiful. The interior's dark wood contrasted perfectly with the white, comfy, inviting furniture and the white curtains covering the open windows and moving in the breeze. Burning candles were placed throughout, and the smell mixed with the scent of jungle flowers and something spicy yet oddly appealing that I didn't recognize. Soft music played in the background, water tinkled from a waterfall feature on one of the walls, and the employees were all pretty elves dressed entirely in white with matching Mona Lisa smiles. I wondered if that smile was a job requirement.

One of the smiling elves approached me. "Ms. Holly? I'm Sage. We're so happy you're here."

To my surprise, she pulled me into a hug. I'm not usually a hugger, and this one lasted about ten seconds too long. Sage was tiny and pretty, with dark hair and eyes and freckles on her nose. She smelled good, too, the same mysterious and spicy aroma I noticed when I came into the spa. But the hugging was a problem. Just when I couldn't take it another second, she released me and gazed at me with a concerned frown on her sweet face.

"Oh, no. You poor dear. You're carrying around a lot of stress and pain, aren't you? I've never felt so much tension in a single body before, but we'll fix this. We'll make it better."

She still kept her hands on my forearms, but I didn't mind so much anymore. "Okay. Thank you."

She linked her arm in mine and led me into the interior area of the spa. "I think you should start with the Eternal Spring Therapeutic massage. First, our masseuse Serene will perform a back and foot exfoliation with a gentle scrub made from jungle plants only found in this area. The Mayans prized them for their healing and therapeutic properties. We found an ancient hidden garden near the temple many years ago." She pointed out the window to the Mayan structure looming close to us. "Secrets were buried in that garden. Many secrets."

Her voice held an odd note. "What kind of secrets?"

"Oh, you know. Herbs. Flowers. The bodies of virgins killed in sacrificial rituals. The usual." She shrugged as if they uncovered the bones of dead virgins daily here. "Back to the massage. After the exfoliation—"

"You're not grinding up the bones of those virgins, are you?"

She laughed. "Of course not," she said, but something in her tone rang false. Before I could question it, she continued with the massage description. "We'll use warm towel compresses and special sacred Belizean heated stones to provide warmth and comfort to your stress points and relax you further. A thorough massage will follow that—"

I interrupted her. "It's only a massage, right?"

"Excuse me?"

"I won't be given an aphrodisiac? You won't make me high by burning something?"

"Absolutely not." She seemed confused. "The massage is amazing. Trust me. And completely natural. You won't be the same elf when Serene finishes with you."

Sage handed me off to Serene, another pretty nature elf, but Serene had arms like Christmas hams. She led me to a dressing room, where I took off all my clothing and wrapped myself in a soft, luxurious robe. Once I was ready, she brought me to a quiet, dimly lit room and started the treatment. My bones felt like jelly when she finished, and I'd never been so calm.

This was followed by a hair mask, a mani-pedi, and a facial. The mud on my face needed an hour to work its magic, so Sage brought me to a large balcony filled with chaise lounges and a fantastic view of the temple. She handed me a drink called a Belizean sunset and planted me in a chair.

"The mask must stay on for one hour. Not a minute more and not a minute less." She set a timer. "I'll be back when this goes off. Try to relax and enjoy the serenity. You've earned it."

I sat back in my chair with a contented sigh. With my hair wrapped in a towel, my face covered in drying mud, and my toes separated by foam so the pedicure would dry properly, I felt pampered. From my vantage point, I could see people entering and exiting the spa, but they couldn't see me. That was a good thing. I was covered in mud, slightly drunk from the Belizean sunset, and blissed out from Serene's massage. That woman knew what she was doing.

I'd finished my second drink, and the timer was about to go off when I noticed a familiar figure leaving the spa. I sat up, wondering if my eyes might be playing tricks on me. Putting down my drink, I got to my feet and hobbled to the balcony's edge. I knew that guy, and it was confirmed when I yelled his name.

"Al Winkle?"

He turned to me, his expression one of surprise mixed with confusion. I understood why. My face was covered in cracking mud, and I may have dribbled some of the Belizean sunset on my white robe. Since it was red, it looked like I had blood on my chest.

He took a step back, tripping on a root. "Who...who are you?"

"That's for me to know and you to find out." Not my best response, but I was buzzed on Belizean sunset and full of endorphins after my massage. I wasn't thinking straight. I pointed a finger at him, hoping I looked threatening. "Don't you dare move. We need to talk."

But Al had never been good at following directions. "Frack this," he said and disappeared straight into the jungle.

SEVENTEEN

I chased Al but couldn't sprint with foam stuck between my toes. He was long gone when I made it to the lobby. I attempted to follow him, but the underbrush was thick, I didn't have shoes on, and the local insects seemed abnormally drawn to my mud mask. When I returned to the spa, I was covered in bug bites, itchy, and disappointed.

Not only that, but I ended up scaring several women waiting for their treatments and causing a minor fiasco with the staff as soon as I reentered the building. They'd been nothing but pleasant to me, but apparently, they weren't used to clients running out of the building and screaming with mud masks still on their faces. I couldn't help it, though. Seeing Al shocked me and losing him felt like a significant setback. But why was he even here in the first place? He did not seem like a spa kind of guy.

Sage took me by the arm and attempted to lead me away from the startled women in the lobby. "Come now, Ms. Holly. Let's finish your treatment, and you can rejoin your lovely new husband."

The thought of Jax made me dig in my heels. I untangled myself from her grip and held up a finger to stop her.

"Wait. Give me a second."

I turned and approached the elf working the front desk. A pleasantly plump elf with a wild mane of curly dark hair, her name tag read Hortense, an odd choice for a nature elf. They usually had hippie names like Rainbow, Sunshine, or Kush. Hortense was unusual, and the Hortense at the front desk looked unsure if she should bolt, assist me, or call security.

I decided I'd better be gentle with her. If I were her, I already would have called security, so I knew her finger was likely hovering over an emergency alert button under her desk. I attempted to feign a relaxed demeanor. I leaned one elbow on the counter and let out a fake little laugh.

"Ha, ha. Excuse me, Hortense. A funny thing happened. An elf left here a few moments ago. Short guy with a bad haircut and the face of a weasel on crack?"

"Al Winkle?" she asked, still looking terrified of me. Not that I blamed her. The bugs had followed me inside, and I suspected a few of them might be attempting to make a nest on my forehead. A chunk of mud fell off my nose and landed on the pristine surface of the registration desk. Hortense winced. I winced, too. The mask was starting to hurt.

"Yes. Al Winkle. What did he want exactly?"

The mask had hardened to the point that it was hard to form words. My mouth no longer moved properly. It was almost like being a ventriloquist, but without the dummy.

It took Hortense a few seconds to translate my garbled words into something logical. "Oh. I'm not sure. He said he was waiting for someone, but he seemed jumpy. He left after only a few minutes."

"Did he say anything else?"

She frowned. The mud felt like a rock. At this point, they were going to have to chisel it off. "Not to me, but I heard him say something as he left. It was along the lines of 'I can't believe this. Where is he?' And he exited the building. And you followed, looking like..." She paused as if trying to come up with the right words to describe my appearance. Sage stepped in.

"Looking like a satisfied spa customer," said Sage in an overly loud and cheerful voice. "Now it's time to get this healing mud mask off your face before it's stuck there. Permanently."

She kept that Mona Lisa smile on her face. I blinked at her in surprise. Well, I tried to blink. One of my eyelids seemed to be malfunctioning. "Are you serious?" I asked. She didn't understand my question. It sounded more like, "Ahhhhh ooooo eeeeeriiiiouuuus?"

"Yes, it is the most amazing sensation, now isn't it?" she asked, pulling me none too gently into the back area of the spa. Once there, she plopped me into a chair and began applying hot compresses to my face. She worked quickly. Time seemed to be of the essence, and she did take out an actual chisel.

"Jiminy Christmas," I said.

She shushed me. "We'll have none of that language here, Ms. Holly. Be quiet. I need to get this off of you. Now."

I followed her directions and shushed. I didn't want to have the mask on my face a moment longer, nor did I want the chisel to slip. It turned out Sage was like a mask removal surgeon. Once she'd gotten the last bit off, she took a long breath and reached for a glass spray bottle on the shelf. She began spraying me, the room, and herself.

"That smells good," I said, inhaling deeply. "What is it?"

"Bug spray," she said, narrowing her eyes at me. "You brought a swarm of gnats with you after your little jungle expedition."

"Sorry," I said, hoping the bug spray wasn't toxic. I'd inhaled enough to do some serious damage.

"It's okay," she said. "It happens. I'm more worried about your skin. I told you the mask had to come off in exactly an hour—not a minute more, and not a minute less. But don't worry. The swelling should be down by tomorrow, and the color of your face will be back to normal in a few days. Hopefully. Your belongings are in the changing room. Please exit through the back of the building. Enjoy the rest of your stay, Ms. Holly."

With that, she left. I stared after her in confusion. The color of my face? What had she meant by that?

I got my answer a few seconds later when I entered the changing room and caught a glimpse of myself in the mirror.

"Oh, frack," I said, repeating the favorite swear word among the nature elves. "I'm green. Great."

I wasn't simply green. I was a weird, glowing, neon green, and covered in bug bites. My face was swollen from the treatment, but the bites began to itch and swell, too. I looked like a red and green Christmas package that had fallen off Santa's sleigh and landed in a dump. I was a total mess. I wanted to hide, but I had to find Jax. If we had any chance of locating Al Winkle, time was of the essence.

I put on my clothing, brushed out my hair, and stuck on my tennis shoes. I wished I had a hoody or something to cover my spotted, green face, but I didn't. Oh, well. I'd looked worse. This wasn't the first time Jax had witnessed me looking like a train wreck. It seemed to be an ongoing theme.

After locating the back door of the salon, I exited and began heading down the path toward the mineral springs. To my surprise, Jax and Ganja were marching up the path toward me. When Jax saw my face, his eyes widened in alarm.

"Tink. What happened?"

"What do you mean?" I asked, just to mess with him.

He took my face in his hands and studied it, his alarm morphing into concern. "Your face is swollen. And green. And you're covered in bites. Are you okay?"

"Mud mask malfunction. Say that ten times fast."

I gave him my signature thumbs up, but I couldn't wink at him. My eyes were too swollen.

Jax shook his head but was more in disbelief than anger this time. That was a good sign. It felt like progress. "How do these things always seem to happen to you?"

"Lucky, I guess."

I expected Ganja to laugh since he always found my problems endlessly amusing, but he didn't. His face was oddly pale, and he ran a worried hand through his hair.

"Ganja? What's going on? Is everything alright?"

"It's Angelica. She's missing. Have you seen her?"

"No, I haven't."

He blew out a breath. "I don't know what's going on. She should have returned from her yoga session hours ago, but no one has heard from her."

"What about her wristband?" I asked, holding up mine.

"It's not functioning," said Ganja. "It stopped working only minutes after we parted ways this morning. I have a bad feeling."

An odd shiver went over my body. I had a bad feeling, too.

Jax and Ganja still had on their swim trunks and T-shirts. They must have been in the mineral springs when they heard about Angelica. They likely bonded at some point because I sensed a change in their dynamics.

Ganja wanted to go back to his room to change. He asked if we could meet up again afterward, and we agreed. After he left, Jax pulled me to the side of the path.

"You haven't seen or heard from Angelica? At all?"

"No, I haven't. But I saw someone else," I said, lowering my voice. "Al Winkle."

Jax blinked in surprise. "Al was here? At the resort?"

I nodded. "I saw him leaving the spa. I chased him, but he ran into the jungle, and I lost him. I'm sorry."

"I guess that explains the bug bites." He gave me a ghost of a smile.

"Bingo. What should we do?" I asked.

"We need to talk," said Jax. "And sort all of this out."

"Good idea," I said, noticing some of the other guests were beginning to take an interest in us. Or maybe they were taking an interest in me. It wasn't every day you saw an elf with a green face and red polka dots. "But let's take this discussion somewhere more private. Can we go back into our room yet?"

Jax nodded. "Cress let me know that they restored it to its former glory, and we can return at our convenience. And Reggie told me he found Felix. The only items in Felix's cache were objects of a personal nature. Objects belonging to you."

I eyed him warily. "What kind of objects?"

"Undergarments." Jax's cheeks reddened slightly. "Your bras, to be precise. And Felix... well, he did things to them.

Reggie assumed you would not want them back, but he promised the resort would replace anything stolen or defaced by the monkeys at the resort."

"Ew. That little jerk had monkey sex with my bras, didn't he?" I wanted to cry. I collected bras the way some girls collected souvenir spoons or postcards. They were my thing. And knowing Felix had his little monkey hands, and possibly other parts, on my stuff pissed me off.

"He did. And apparently, Felix is into cross-dressing now because he's taken to wearing your bras and won't give them back. Sorry, Tink."

I waved a hand. "That's the final insult in this whole debacle of a day. Let's go back to our place. We need to talk, and we need to pull our act together. Before Ganja shows up."

Jax scowled at me. "Why do I sense there is something you haven't told me yet?"

"Because there is, Jax," I said, feeling both sad and resigned. "Because there always is."

EIGHTEEN

The room looked like wild monkeys had never ransacked it. Other than my missing bras (and, of course, Felix took all my best ones), the place felt fresh, clean, and full of luxurious touches. They even left us food by way of apology, a gorgeous tray of bread, cheese, fruit, dessert, and coffee. It sat on a small table near the window with two chairs. Jax poured the coffee while I grabbed a plate and dug into the food.

I was starving, as usual. I hadn't eaten any lunch, and this morning had taken a lot out of me. Jax handed me a cup of coffee, went into the bathroom to change into dry clothing, and then sat in the chair across from me. He studied me as I ate. I paused in mid-bite of my baguette.

"What is it?"

"Your face." He reached over the table and touched my cheek, wincing slightly. "It's pretty swollen. And green. Are you sure you're okay? Should we go to the emergency room again?"

I waved the baguette as I shook my head. "I'm good. Sage from the spa told me my face should return to normal in no time. At least it isn't itchy anymore. And the bug spray I ingested was organic and non-toxic. I'm sure that's fine, too."

He frowned. "Bug spray—?

I waved the baguette again before taking another bite. It took a few minutes of chewing before I could speak. "No need to worry about that, but there is something I need to tell you. It's important." I paused, trying to figure out a good way to explain. I couldn't find one, so I dove right in. "As Scarlet lay dying on the club floor, she gave me something. A flash drive."

"I know."

I nearly choked on my baguette. "You do? But how?" I frowned as it clicked into place. "It was Grandma Gingersnap, wasn't it?"

"Yes, your grandmother told me. She was concerned due to your hair-brained scheme to steal it from Ganja. And she was right."

"Why didn't you say something sooner?'

"Why didn't you?" he asked, his expression solemn.

I bit my lip. "Uh, because I knew my plan to steal it from Ganja would work, but I had a feeling you would disapprove. I also didn't want to get you into any more trouble. I'm sorry, Jax. I should have told you. But I'm telling you now, so I guess that counts for something, right?"

I nearly gave him a thumbs up but managed to stop myself. He seemed oddly hurt, which was far worse than him being angry.

"I don't want to psychoanalyze you, but I see a pattern here. It's one of self-sabotage. It seems like a habit, something you may not even be aware that you're doing, but you demonstrate it when you make such poor choices."

"Story of my life."

"Well, it's time to change that. It's time to face your demons and grow up."

I wasn't up for a lecture at the moment. I attempted to narrow my puffy eyes at him but couldn't quite pull it off. "Great. Now you sound like Grandma Gingersnap."

"Your grandmother is right." He shook his head sadly. "But we need to stay on task. Ganja is on his way here, Angelica could be in terrible danger, and we don't have time to figure you out. That would take years, not minutes."

"True. What do you suggest we do?"

"First, no more secrets between us. Deal?"

That was easy. "Deal."

"Secondly, we need to do a recap," he said, ticking off fingers. "Scarlet gave you a flash drive as she lay dying on the floor of the club, and Ganja stole it from you minutes later."

I nodded. "Yep."

"And Ganja still doesn't realize that you're Mistle Ho?"

I shook my head. "I don't think so. I was masked, and I had on a wig. He mentioned that I looked familiar on the plane, but he assumed it was because he'd seen me in *Elf* magazine."

Jax sat back in his chair, his expression pensive. "That might work in our favor. Ganja and I had a long talk today while bathing in the hot springs."

"Bathing?"

An image came into my mind of Jax and Ganja scrubbing each other's backs with soapy sponges. Something in my expression must have betrayed my thoughts because Jax narrowed his eyes at me.

"Really, Tink?"

I shrugged. "I can't help it. So you and Gan-Gan were sudsing each other up, and....?"

"We were doing no such thing. Please stop purposefully misunderstanding me." He took a long, deep breath in what I could only assume was an effort to calm himself. He may have counted to ten as he tried not to lose it. I gave him points for effort.

"Sorry. What did you and Ganja discuss?"

"Lots of things. He seems like a reasonable person, and he might be willing to help us." Jax's cell phone buzzed with a text, and Jax got to his feet. "He's here now."

"What should we do? What should we say?"

Jax paused. "We'll play it by ear. That always works so well for us."

A tap sounded at the door. Jax opened it, and Ganja walked inside. He'd changed into long pants and a long-sleeved shirt, and his face was lined with worry.

"I spoke with the hotel again. They've already sent a team out into the jungle to look for Angelica. They say that perhaps she wandered off the path and got lost. I disagree."

"What do you think is going on?" asked Jax.

Ganja ran a hand through his hair. "I think it's because of me. Someone may have kidnapped her. Or worse."

He seemed so genuinely distraught that I put a hand on his arm. "Or it might be unrelated. Have you gotten a ransom note?"

"No."

Jax pondered the situation. "Is there anyone you think might have it out for you?"

Ganja laughed, but there was no humor in it. "The list is long. It would be hard to narrow it down."

"Is Al Winkle on it?" I asked.

Ganja seemed surprised. "He is, actually. Why do you mention him?"

"Because he's here. I saw him earlier today at the spa."

Ganja sank into a chair. "Oh, this is not good. Al owes me money. He could be planning to use Angelica as a bargaining chip. Or it could be payback. His girlfriend died recently, and Al blames me for it."

"Ruby?"

"Yes." He shook his head. "I got Ruby a job working at one of the charities I support. She was doing well there, or so I thought. Then she died of an overdose. I didn't even know she was using. In truth, it wasn't my fault, and Al knows it, but it's easier to blame me. There is no reasoning with Al. He will forever see himself as a victim. He cannot admit his role in not protecting Ruby better, or his self-sabotaging, destructive behavior."

Al sounded a bit like me. Except I admitted it when I was wrong. Usually. And I didn't kidnap anyone. Usually.

"What can we do?" asked Jax.

Ganja sighed. "You both work for the EBI. Normally, I wouldn't ask, but I'm desperate. You have resources I don't have. Will you help me?"

My gaze locked on Jax's. We didn't have resources and were both in hot water at the Bureau. I hoped I was doing the right thing here. It felt right, but Jax had just pointed out that I was not the queen of good decisions.

"We're not here on official business, to be clear, but we'll help you," I said. "We need something in return, though."

Ganja nodded, his expression tired. "I assumed that would be the case. What do you want? Names? Dates? Places? Christmas cake?"

The last one was tempting, but I shook my head. "No. We want the flash drive. The one you took from me the night Scarlet died."

At first, he seemed confused, but comprehension dawned in his eyes. "You're Mistle Ho?"

"In the flesh."

He let out a laugh. "I should have known. Only you would be crazy enough to try to stop me from leaving the club. Now that I know you, I realize it's a total Tink Holly move." He glanced at Jax, and back at me, as if attempting to assess our sincerity. He must have liked what he saw. "Fine. But why do you want that flash drive so badly?"

"Because we think it could help us figure out who killed Scarlet and why," said Jax. "We suspect Al Winkle."

Ganja didn't seem shocked by this revelation. "I wondered if that might have been the case," he said. "Although Al doesn't seem the type. He's a blackmailer and a slimeball, but he's hardly a murderer."

"Sometimes people change," I said, echoing his words about Angelica.

"True," he said. "I'm sorry Scarlet died because of it. She was a friend like Ruby. I've known them for years. I'm friends with Scarlet's brother, as well."

"Red?" I asked.

"Yep. He used to work for me. He's an accountant. But after I went legitimate, I didn't need Red's special brand of creative accounting anymore, and we parted ways." He sighed. "And four years later, his sister and his niece are dead. He adored them. It must have rocked him to his core. Of course, I want to help. I'll get you the flash drive, but on one condition."

"What is it?"

He paused as if weighing his words. "The flash drive is password protected. I don't know what's on it. Do you promise to use only what is related to Scarlet's death and Al? Because otherwise I can't give it to you. I can't risk incriminating myself or one of my associates for something relatively minor when you're looking for a murderer."

My gaze met Jax. He nodded. "Agreed. You have my word. I'm only interested in the murder, Ganja. And the drugs."

"It's a deal," said Ganja.

"One more question." I lifted a finger. "What size shoes do you wear, Ganja?"

He seemed perplexed. "Thirteen."

I glanced down at his feet. They were huge. "Wow. Impressive. And good news."

"Excuse me?" asked Ganja. "Why?"

Jax followed my train of thought. "She's right. It is good news. Because you aren't the one who broke into our room."

He explained about the footprint. Ganja listened attentively. "What were they after?" he asked.

I sighed. "I wish we knew. It must have been something important." I rubbed my temples. "First, I set up the undercover operation that got Scarlet killed. And I lost the flash drive, but that was really thanks to you."

Ganja lifted his hands in defeat. "Apologies. I saw Al pass it to Scarlet. He kept giving me weird looks as he did it."

"Al always gives weird looks."

"You're right, but these seemed especially weird. That's why I took the flash drive. I thought he could be up to something."

"Al is usually up to something," I said with a sigh. "This keeps getting worse and worse. Now Angelica is missing. And, judging by what happened to Scarlet..."

I didn't finish my sentence. We all knew Angelica might be in terrible danger right now. I didn't say the words out loud, but I knew they were thinking it, too. To my surprise, Jax reached over and squeezed my shoulder.

"Stop blaming yourself, Tink. Move on."

"He's right," said Ganja. "Scarlet's death wasn't your fault. This feels like a professional hit."

"It feels like that to me, too," said Jax. "But why would someone put a hit on Scarlet?"

"That's what bothers me," I said. "She was pretty much a model citizen. Never arrested. Never in trouble. It's not like she was..."

My voice faded as the wheels began turning in my head. Ganja eyed me curiously. "It's not like she was what, Tink?"

"It's not like she was you." I swallowed hard. "What if we've had this all wrong? What if Scarlet wasn't the target? What if someone was trying to kill you, Ganja?"

"I do have a lot of enemies from the old days," he said. "Some more dangerous than others. It makes sense."

"And Scarlet was in the wrong place at the wrong time?" Jax rubbed his jaw. "I see where you're going, but that would mean we've been focusing on the incorrect person."

"Exactly. And I know there was no bullet, but something zipped past my head. It cut my ear." I stood in front of Ganja. "Let's work this out. I'm on stage. Something comes from behind—"

"From the offstage area—behind the curtain. Someone could have been there," said Jax.

"Bingo. And some sort of bullet that wasn't a bullet nicks me and goes through Scarlet's neck. If Scarlet hadn't stepped into that exact spot, it could have hit you, Ganja. You were sitting right behind her."

"And the angle of Scarlet's wound supports that theory. I read the autopsy report." Jax's dark eyes grew pensive. "It entered the front of her neck nearly an inch higher than the exit wound. We'll have to look at the club again, but if I'm remembering correctly, and if the object that killed her came from behind Tink on the stage, that means the perpetrator had to be someone tall or they were standing on top of something."

"You're right," I said. "The angle bugged me before, but I focused on other things. Like how I screwed up and got Scarlet killed."

"And now you know that's not true," said Ganja. "Whether or not you'd set up that undercover operation, Scarlet and I would have still been at the club together that night. Al Winkle would have still been there, too. And the miners. And the other dancers. And the other customers. Let's blame the murderer, not ourselves."

His words echoed the words Scarlet's mom had said to me. Coming from Ganja, however, they helped.

"Thank you." I turned to Jax. "What do we do now? We need to find Angelica. Where do we start?"

"We start where the trail ends. Where we last saw Angelica." He checked his watch. "We still have time before the sun sets. I'm going to call Reggie for help. He knows this place, and if he can track Felix, the monkey, he can track Angelica."

"Felix the monkey?" asked Ganja.

"Don't ask," I said. "He's a bra-stealing menace."

Jax pulled out his phone. "You'll need to get changed. Wear pants and something with long sleeves. We're going into the jungle."

I considered my wardrobe options. The only pants I had were leggings, which made my butt look big, but finding Angelica outweighed embarrassment over my butt at this point. I grabbed my things and went to the bathroom to change. That's when I realized the only long-sleeved shirt I had was sheer and white, and the only bras Felix had not taken were the red ones.

"Jiminy Christmas," I muttered under my breath. At least no one would be looking at my butt. The red push-up bra under the white, filmy shirt solved that problem. Also, if I hadn't already told Ganja I was Mistle Ho, he would have caught on after seeing the red bra, but there was nothing to be done about it. The only jacket I had was the white one from Grandma Gingersnap's suit that I'd worn on the airplane. She'd kill me if I wore it in the jungle. Or her faux fur stole. If I wore that, I'd die of heat exhaustion, or some jungle animal would kill me. At least the red bra might scare away predators.

I glanced at the mirror and groaned. My face was still puffy and pale green. The bug bites weren't as swollen, but it looked like I had pin pricks on my face. My boobs seemed enormous, and every bit of the red bra was visible under my shirt. The only good thing? My hair shone in the light of the bathroom. Whatever treatment they'd used on that had worked. If only the mud mask hadn't messed up my face, and if the monkeys hadn't stolen my undergarments, I would have looked pretty hot.

"Tink. Are you nearly ready?"

I heard the impatience in Jax's voice. I pulled my gloriously shiny hair into a bun and prepared to face the music. They both stared at me in shock when I opened the bathroom door. Jax, who wore sensible, long-sleeved, jungle-hiking clothing, gasped.

"What do you have on?" he asked.

I crossed my arms over my chest self-consciously. "Felix took all my other bras. He only left the red ones."

"It's a sign," said Ganja. "From Scarlet. She wants us to work together to solve this."

When I glanced at his face, his expression surprised me. "You're serious, aren't you?"

He placed a big hand on my arm. "A nature elf never kids about signs and omens, *bèl fi*. This can only mean one thing."

"What?"

"We're moving in the right direction. Now let's go and find Angelica."

NINETEEN

The jungle scared me. I'd grown up in a land of snow and ice. I wasn't used to all the birds and insects, the heat bothered me, and even the greenery made me feel claustrophobic. I jumped at every noise, got stuck in the mud twice, and seemed to attract everything that stung or bit. After the third time Ganja had to pull me away before I stepped on a snake or got caught in a prickly vine, or accidentally ate poisonous berries, Jax let out a sigh.

"Maybe we should take you back to the resort, Tink."

I shook my head. "No way. The red bra was a sign. I'm supposed to be here."

Reggie frowned in confusion, but my words earned a broad smile from Ganja. "The *gyal* is right. She needs to stay. We should keep going together."

And keep going we did. We started where Angelica's wristband had last pinged, but after thoroughly combing through the area, we couldn't find any indication that Angelica had been there. Further up the path, however, we located her wristband. It sat in the mud and smashed beyond repair.

"Should we go to where she was supposed to do yoga?" I asked, swatting at the swarm of gnats surrounding my face. They seemed abnormally attracted to me. Reggie said it always happened to Christmas elves.

"It's because you're all so sweet," he said with a grin. "Or maybe it's all the cookies."

"My vote is for the cookies. We aren't really that nice," I said, choking as a bug flew into my mouth. I needed to stop talking.

Reggie waited until I stopped choking and spitting out the bug to answer. "It wouldn't hurt to look there. Are you sure you're up for this? It's a climb."

Unable to speak, I gave him a thumbs up. In this case, the thumbs up didn't feel awkward at all. It worked.

The path was narrow and twisting. Getting there was a workout. I didn't know how Angelica planned to do yoga after this hike, but she seemed fit. My only exercise involved stumbling down the block every morning to get a peppermint mocha (with extra whipped cream and sprinkles on top) and my recent foray into pole dancing. I did not have much experience with hiking or jungles, and I wished I hadn't brought up the red bra as a sign I should be here. I was exhausted and ready to give up when Reggie pointed to a small clearing.

"This is the spot."

We stepped into the peaceful, idyllic area. The sun shone down on us, and pretty purple flowers covered the ground. I reached down to touch one, and Ganja stopped me.

"Those are mountain lotus. They'll put you in a meditative trance if you touch them with your bare skin. Great for yoga, but not for finding Angelica."

I put my hands on my hips. "Even the flowers here are

trying to drug me? Is everything in this country hazardous? So far, we were given an aphrodisiac in a cake and inhaled some mind-altering substance while we meditated. And there was also the mud mask." I pointed to my face. "Although that was kind of my fault. I didn't follow the instructions. But facials don't normally turn me into an ogre. I feel that's a bit negligent on the spa's part, too."

"Not negligent. It's a cultural difference. We follow old traditions here," said Ganja. "We're in tune with nature. What you call 'drugging' is what we see as accessing a higher level of understanding of the universe. And there was nothing given to you that would change you or make you act in a way inconsistent with your truest self. The cures and treatments here bring out your inner longings. The only thing they do is make it impossible for you to hide what you honestly desire."

As Ganja chatted with Reggie, my gaze locked on Jax's. Was what Ganja said true? I'd thought we could blame the drugs for our behavior, but was that the case, or had this experience brought the truth about how Jax and I felt about each other to the surface?

"Tink, I—" Whatever Jax meant to say was interrupted when Reggie and Ganja found something amidst the carpet of mountain lotus blossoms. It was a small, pink ribbon.

I gasped. "That's Angelica's. She had it in her hair this morning."

It felt like so much time had passed since I spoke with Angelica on the way to yoga this morning. In reality, it had happened only hours ago. We'd seen her before our meditation session had started at eight, and it was now close to five.

Reggie lifted it carefully. He had gloves on his hands. "She made it here. She didn't get lost. Not on the way to the clearing, at least."

Ganja stared at the ribbon. "What could have happened to her?"

"I don't know." Reggie took out his phone and called the front desk. When he hung up, his face looked bleak.

"I spoke with Fern at the front desk. Our staff has been searching for her, but with no luck. They called the police. Night will be falling soon, and the jungle is a dangerous place at night."

"We need to act quickly," said Jax. "What are our next steps?"

I walked around the perimeter of the clearing as the others talked about strategies for finding Angelica. We were running out of time. Once the sun went down, we'd have to stop searching. And the idea of Angelica being out in the jungle all night alone scared me. She was no survivalist. She seemed even less capable of handling the jungle than me, and I was pretty low on the jungle survival totem pole.

I couldn't do many things well, but I was observant and felt liked we'd missed something. "Low on the totem pole," I said softly as I crouched down, careful not to touch the mountain lotus with my bare skin. If Angelica had been doing yoga, she'd have her mat on the ground. If she'd fallen into a trance-like state, it would be easy for someone to sneak up on her.

Although not apparent initially, I found one area of the ground that appeared to have slightly compressed flowers. The area was rectangular in shape and the perfect size for a yoga mat.

As the others yammered on about our next steps, I studied the rectangle and realized it was next to where we'd found the pink ribbon. I interrupted them.

"Excuse me, guys. I found something."

"What?" asked Jax.

I showed him the rectangle. "Her yoga mat was here. She took off the ribbon and set it next to her mat when she started her practice." I glanced up and noticed the underbrush had been trampled at the side of the clearing opposite the path we'd taken to arrive here. "And someone either came from that direction or left in that direction."

Reggie studied the spot I'd indicated. "You're right. How did you notice that?"

I shrugged. "I pay attention. What should we do?"

Ganja lifted a hand to indicate the trampled brush. "Follow where that leads?"

Reggie called the hotel to let them know exactly where we were, and he asked them to check that our wristbands were operational. Once he confirmed our bands were all working, he pulled a machete from a pack he wore on his back.

"We'll have to go slowly to follow the path they made through the brush," he said. "Stay close."

He was right. It was slow going. Reggie took his time, analyzing each step. We walked in a straight line—Reggie, Ganja, me, and Jax taking up the rear. Jax kept his hand on the small of my back, a reassuring gesture that made me feel safe and protected. I hadn't realized I needed those things, but I hadn't realized much about Jax and me.

Thinking about Ganja's words, about how the aphrodisiac and whatever Lily Garland burned at the meditation session would only amplify what already existed, made me pause. Something inside me knew he'd spoken the truth. I felt it. Just like I felt this thing between Jax and me.

I'd had one serious boyfriend my whole life—my old neighbor and close friend Winter Snow. We'd known each other forever, and it had been something comfortable and predictable.

Well, mostly predictable.

But Win and I were the same. Two halves of a whole. Jax and I were opposites, and yet we were like two halves of a whole as well. In a different way, and yet I still felt complete when I was with him. He stimulated my mind. He made me see things differently. And he turned me on, but that part was almost secondary. Jax could turn anyone on. He was a good guy in bad guy packaging, and everything about him worked for me. His mind. His dry sense of humor. The involuntary sound he made deep in his throat when I kissed him.

Thinking about that sound made me trip on a tree root. Jax grabbed me by the hips, holding me steady, and pulled me closer to him. I let out an involuntary sigh, and his grip tightened on me.

I wanted him, and he wanted me—even when my face was a weird shade of green and covered in spots. He had it bad if he wanted me when I looked like this. Did it have to be so complicated?

I was so focused on Jax and his hands that I didn't notice when Ganja and Reggie came to a stop. We'd reached another clearing, but what loomed in front of us surprised me.

"Altun Ha?"

The Mayan structure rose out of the forest like a giant stone mountain. Everything about it drew me closer—the broad steps leading up the side, the perfect beauty and symmetry of it, and the mystery of it as well.

"The trail ends here. We can't follow it any longer," said Reggie. "There are too many footprints, both human and elven."

"That's disappointing," said Jax. "But we should still take a look around."

As we crossed the spacious, green lawn toward the most prominent building, the Temple of the Masonry Altar, I stared at it in awe. "What was this building used for? I'm assuming virgins were sacrificed at some point, but what other purpose did it serve?"

Ganja answered me. "It played a part in religious ceremonies and virgin sacrifices, but it was much more. Archeologists found seven layers of tombs under the central stairway. And they discovered the famous jade head of Altun Ha here, too."

"The jade head of Altun Ha?" I asked.

"It depicted Kinich Ahau, the Mayan sun god, but he had oddly pointy ears."

I let out a laugh. "The Mayan sun god was a nature elf?"

Ganja shook his head. "No, the jade head looks like a nature elf. But that was long before the veil between our worlds was established. Maybe he was a nature elf. Or maybe not. Who knows?"

I liked the idea of the Mayan sun god being a nature elf. As I watched the humans milling about and exploring Altun Ha, I experienced something strange. I felt, for a moment, as if our two worlds (both elven and human), connected here in some mystical way. And even if I was here for a terrible reason, the sight of this magnificent, ancient structure still inspired me.

Jax seemed awed by it as well. "It's so beautiful," he said. "But if someone brought Angelica here, why? What could be the reasoning?"

We stood side by side, staring up at Altun Ha, as if the structure itself could provide the answers to his questions. And that's when something odd happened.

A small human child, walking toward Altun Ha with

his parents, came to a dead stop right in front of me. I shifted uncomfortably, knowing he couldn't see me. The veil stopped him from doing that. And yet he stared directly at me, his dark eyes huge in his little face.

I grabbed Jax's arm, and that's when the little boy spoke.

"Who is that lady?" he asked, pointing at me. "And why is she all green?"

TWENTY

"The veil is down," said Jax. "We need to leave. Now."

Sometimes, human children could see us. It had happened before. They possessed a magical innocence and a sensitivity that even the veil couldn't protect us from. But not only the little boy stared at us. His parents and other adults did as well.

"This is bad," I said as we walked away from Altun Ha as quickly as we could. "What is going on?"

Ganja glanced over his shoulder. We'd reached the edge of the rainforest. The humans who'd stared at us only moments before looked around in confusion.

"What happened?" asked the mother of the little boy. "Where did they go?"

I heaved a sigh of relief. "It's okay. They can't see us. The veil is working. It must have been a glitch."

Jax shook his head. "That was no glitch."

"I agree." Reggie pulled out his phone. "This is the path back to the resort," he said, indicating a winding green trail. "Follow it. I'm going to get security here to see where the breach of the veil is and how we can contain it. This is bad.

I've worked here half my life and never seen anything like this."

"What about Angelica?" asked Ganja.

Reggie shook his head, his dreads swinging. "We need to fix the veil first. This could have worldwide consequences. We'll search for her as soon as possible."

Ganja looked like he might protest. I touched his arm. "He's right. Let's go back, regroup, and make a plan."

He grudgingly agreed, but he obviously wanted to stay and search, breach or no breach. I leaned closer to him. "The flash drive. Scarlet. Al Winkle. Ruby. Angelica. And now the veil. It can't be a coincidence. We have to figure it out. We're missing something, Ganja. I feel it."

He nodded. "You're right, but you promise you won't give up? You'll help me find her?"

"Of course we will."

He let me lead him down the path, but he kept looking over his shoulder as if Angelica might appear at any second. "I feel it, too," he said. "We're missing something. But I also feel like Angelica is close."

"We'll find her," I said, squeezing his arm. "I swear it to you."

Jax nodded. "We won't rest until she's back and she's safe."

When we reached the resort, Ganja went to his room to get the flash drive. Jax and I headed back to the un-honeymoon suite. The entrance to our fancy treehouse faced the rainforest and Altun Ha. A balcony wrapped around the whole place, and the stairs to enter (along with the hoisting device and swing) were in the back, facing the resort. We climbed the steps, and we must have done it quietly. We were deep in thought and trying to figure out our next steps, which was why we didn't notice the guy on our balcony until we were nearly on top of him.

"Al Winkle?"

Al, who'd been using a knife to jimmy open the door, jumped back in surprise. "Oh, frack."

"My sentiments exactly," said Jax.

He took a step forward, and Al waved the knife at us threateningly. "Stay right there. No one else needs to get hurt."

"You're right, Al," I said, trying to remain calm. "What happened to Angelica?"

"Angelica?" He frowned at me. "What happened to your face?"

"Bad spa day. Irrelevant. Where is she, Al?"

Al let out a laugh. "I don't have to tell you anything. I'm the one with the knife. Or did you forget?"

He lifted the knife higher. At that moment, I heard rustling in the trees. Felix, the monkey, flew out, wearing my favorite pink lace bra, and attacked Al. He wrapped his body around Al's upraised arm and bit down hard on his hand. Al screamed, dropping the knife. Felix made a triumphant howler monkey noise, grabbed the knife off the balcony, and scampered up the tree.

"Great. Now the monkey is armed," I said.

"But at least Al isn't." Jax's voice was low and held a deadly quality to it. Al must have heard it, too. His eyes widened in fear.

"Look. I came here to get the flash drive. It doesn't belong to you. I need to return it so no one else gets hurt."

Jax stepped forward, his gaze locked on Al's face. "It doesn't belong to you either."

"I'm the one who gave it to Scarlet, but I never should have gotten involved. It was a huge mistake, and I knew better. These are powerful elves. Like incredibly powerful. People are dying, and now more people are going to die. Please don't do this. Just give me back the flash drive so I can make it all stop."

Al backed up, but he was now pressed against the balcony railing. He had nowhere to go. He shot a panicked look over the edge of the balcony. The ground seemed quite far away.

"Be careful, Al," I said. "We can work this out."

He ran a hand over his gaunt face. Although he was half Christmas Elf, Al didn't sparkle. And although he was half nature elf, he didn't radiate a calm aura. He was a twitchy mess and a low life, but something in his expression made me feel sorry for him.

"I loved Ruby. You know that, right? She was the only good thing that ever happened to me," he said. "And I had nothing against Scarlet. She wasn't my biggest fan, but I knew she only wanted to protect her daughter. I wanted to protect Ruby, too. I never wished harm on either of them."

"Of course, you didn't. Things happen. We can make this right, Al. We can make everything better."

"By arresting me and sending me to the coal mines?" he asked with a bitter laugh. "You know what it's like there, Tink. You did hard time. For a nature elf like me, it's a death sentence. To be trapped underground, with no sky, no sun, nothing green. It's a living nightmare." He nodded toward Jax. "I suppose you know that already."

"I do," he said. Jax didn't move, but every muscle in his body was tight as if waiting for the right moment. "But it's better to turn yourself in. We can fix this."

"Nope," he said with a shudder. "No one can fix this. I'm in deep, and there is no going back. You may as well kill me now."

"Don't say that. You have options, Al. We can make this right."

"Can you? I don't think so, Tink. But I appreciate the thought." When he turned and stared at me, I realized he'd made some sort of decision. "I'm going to leave now, and we're going to pretend this never happened. I don't want to put you in danger. I don't want anyone else to die."

His words sent a tremor of fear over me. Jax took a step forward, but I held him back. "How are you going to get out of here, Al?" I asked. "You're trapped."

He pointed to a vine. "No. I can use that vine. Swing out of here. Like a monkey."

I shook my head. "No, Al, it's too dangerous. You'll fall."

"Maybe. Maybe not." He seemed suddenly calm. He even gave me a little smile. "I know you think I killed Scarlet, but it wasn't me. I never meant for any of this to happen. Tell my mom I'm sorry if I don't make it out of this alive. And tell Flo I'm sorry, too."

He reached for the vine. Felix had used it effectively to swing over to our balcony, but even I could tell it wouldn't be strong enough to hold Al.

"Al, no—" I said, but it was too late. Al grabbed the vine and leaped off the balcony. Jax reached for him but grabbed only air. We heard a snapping sound as the vine broke, and we both stared down at the ground in horror, but Al wasn't there. He'd disappeared.

Ganja chose that moment to walk down the path. "What's going on?" he asked, looking up at us.

"Al Winkle was here. He fell off our balcony. We didn't push him."

I have no idea why I felt the need to add the last part. It seemed appropriate for some reason. I couldn't figure out what had happened. The top of the vine still swayed above us, but it was like Al had disappeared into thin air.

Ganja tilted his head and studied us. "You didn't push him? I've heard that story before. Where did he go? I mean after you didn't push him?"

"No idea," I said. "He disappeared."

"Elves don't just disappear," said Ganja, studying the clearing.

"This one did."

We scrambled down to join Ganja. There was no trace of Al anywhere. I thought I caught a glimpse of something wavering and shimmering in the jungle, but I couldn't tell if the heat made it look that way or if I'd actually seen something.

"Did you see that? I asked.

Jax nodded. "Another glitch in the veil, which means Al could be anywhere."

Ganja wiped a hand over his face. "You're right. And Al is half nature elf. If he wants to get lost in the jungle, no one will be able to find him. Not without considerable effort, at least. And we don't have time for that right now."

"Why?"

"There is something you need to see." He pulled a note out of his pocket. "I found this when I returned to my room a few moments ago."

I unfolded the paper. What I read sent shivers up my spine.

We have your girlfriend. She's alive—for now. If you want her to stay that way, you must do as we ask. Wait for further instructions. We will contact you when the moon is full.

"The moon is full?" I frowned. "When is that?"

"Tomorrow night."

"But why are they waiting for the full moon?"

Ganga shrugged. "For nature elves, the moon cycles are important. Even for Mayans, the moon was nearly as significant as the sun. They followed a lunar calendar. Nature elves do as well."

"So whoever kidnapped her is a nature elf?"

"That's possible. But the moon cycles are important to the other tribes as well. Water elves due to the tides. Air elves due to moon magic and moon rituals. The only elves who don't seem to put importance on the moon are dark elves and Christmas elves."

"You can't place importance on something you never see," said Jax.

I thought about him growing up underground, which made me sad. "Christmas elves are oblivious." I glanced at Ganja. "I guess we have to wait until tomorrow night?"

"Yes, but there is something else." He paused. "The flash drive is gone."

I put my face in my hands. "You're kidding, right?"

"Unfortunately, I'm not. My room was ransacked like yours. It must have happened while we were searching for Angelica. The room was fine when I changed my clothes a few hours ago."

"Someone is watching us," said Jax.

"Maybe it was Al," said Ganja. "He gave the flash drive to Scarlet. Maybe he saw me take it from you, Tink."

"Maybe. Al was here looking for the flash drive. He asked us for it before he jumped. I mean, first, he threatened us with a knife, and asked for the flash drive. Felix the monkey stole the knife, and that was when Al jumped. After he told us he never met to hurt Scarlet." I frowned. "Was that a confession? Had he killed Scarlet by accident? I'm so confused. And it's getting worse by the minute. We don't even know if Scarlet was the intended victim or not anymore, and we still don't know what killed her. It's a muddle."

"You're right," said Jax. "But I'm afraid most of those answers disappeared with Al Winkle."

"No, because I know where Al might have gone." I lifted my chin, the wheels turning in my head. "To his mother—Petunia Winkle. And I know exactly where to find her."

<h1 style="text-align:center">TWENTY-ONE</h1>

"You knew Al's mother's address and didn't tell me?" asked Jax as we rode together in a jungle jeep to Petunia Winkle's farm. The vehicle had big tires, and the roof was open to the sky. A soft top was rolled up against the back seat that we could pull on in case of rain. I held onto one of the roll bars for dear life as Jax sped over the bumpy, rutted dirt road. If not for my seatbelt, I would have been airborne, and I think my soul left my body at one point.

"Dude, slow down. I honestly forgot. I found the address in Chief Sleigh's office. But after getting roofied, stoned, and robbed by monkeys and having an allergic reaction to just about everything in the nature elf world, I was kind of distracted. I was focused on Angelica. Give me a break."

My face was still green from the mud mask, and my hair had come loose from my bun. I must have looked pretty pathetic because Jax slowed down and gave me a sympathetic wince. "Does it still itch?"

"Not as much."

It didn't itch at all, but I was milking it since it appeared far worse than it felt. I'd taken an antihistamine before bed last night and passed out. I seemed less swollen this morning, and my eyes weren't as puffy, but I still had an odd greenish cast to my skin.

"I don't know. The green suits you," he said, giving me a wink.

I shot him a dirty look. "You're hilarious. At least my grandmother doesn't know about this. That would be the worst—" At that moment, my phone rang. It was Grandma Gingersnap, and she wanted to FaceTime me. "Jiminy Christmas. I swear that woman has radar. What should I do?"

He shrugged. "Stop swearing and answer the phone. How bad could it be?"

I sighed because he had no idea, but I did as he suggested. I answered the phone. I had no choice.

"Hi, Grandma."

She gasped as soon as she saw me. "Tink Holly. What have you done to your face?"

"Long story. I had an allergic reaction to a mud mask at the spa. I should go back to my normal color in a day or two. Hopefully." I cleared my throat. "How are you?"

She stared at me. She didn't answer at first. It took her ten seconds to recover from the shock of seeing my face.

"Listen to me, young lady. You need to go to the doctor. Now."

"I've already been to the emergency room. Not for this. For a different allergic reaction. That was to an aphrodisiac." I wrinkled my nose. "Pretend I didn't say that last part. My point is I have antihistamines, and I'm totally fine."

Jax hit a bump, and I flew into the air, nearly losing my phone. It fell on the floor of the jeep. When I picked it up and faced my grandmother again, she was fuming.

"I would like to speak with Jax. Now."

I turned the phone so she could yell at Jax for a few minutes. He waited until the tirade was over, reassured her he was taking care of me, and told her in the calmest tones possible that I would not suffer any long-term effects due to the mud mask.

My grandmother let out a humph. "She'd better not. I want her to be back to her regular color when she comes home. Is that understood?"

"Yes, ma'am," he said.

I turned the phone back to me. "Now that we're done talking about my face, I need to ask you a question. Grandma, have you ever heard about the veil malfunctioning?"

She frowned. "There was something that happened years ago when I worked at Elf Central. But it wasn't exactly a malfunction."

"What was it?"

"First of all, I want to be clear. This is second-hand information."

She seemed embarrassed. I had no idea why. "Who does it come from?"

"Well, I told you I was dating a dark elf at the time."

"Yes. Zakar of Neslos."

Jax looked at me in shock. "Your grandmother dated Zakar of Neslos?"

"In her misspent youth," I said. "Go on, Grandma. What happened?"

"My youth was not misspent, and Zakar and I only dated briefly. But during that time, there was an issue with the veil. Zakar told me about it. I guess certain portals lead from the human world to the elf world. Sometimes these portals are opened by accident, like when a human stumbles through a weak area in the veil. A wrong place, wrong time sort of thing. This has happened a handful of times and was always taken care of quickly and efficiently. The human's memory was wiped, they were sent back to the other side of the veil, and the glitch was repaired." She paused. "But when I was dating Zakar, a different sort of breach happened."

"That's what she said." I let out a snort. My grandmother narrowed her eyes at me, and I apologized. "Please continue. What sort of breach?"

"Some elves were using the portals to smuggle things in from the human world. Alcohol. Painkillers. Designer handbags. Glitter."

"Glitter?" asked Jax.

"Glitter is like catnip for Christmas elves," I explained. "We can never have enough of it. And the humans produced it much more cheaply than we did."

"That's correct," said Grandma Gingersnap. "But we've learned better methods now. We make our own glitter. This was nearly fifty years ago, but that breach had a big impact on our society."

"Why?"

"They were smuggling coca seeds and planting them illegally in the nature elf community. That's how the candicocane problem began. The breach started where you are right now."

That made me ask one more question. "What would a breach look like? I mean to the naked eye?"

She considered my question. "Well, I've never seen it, but I've heard it shimmers and ripples. Like the surface of a pond when there's a gentle breeze."

"That's what I was afraid of. Thank you, Grandma. We'll be in touch soon. I'll be home before you know it."

After promising my grandmother I would not get lost in the rainforest or put anything else on my face, I shut off my phone.

"You think Al crossed through the veil?" asked Jax.

"What better way to disappear?"

"I guess. Does that mean we won't get any answers?"

I tapped my phone against my chin. "Not necessarily. Petunia must know something. Why else would Al want us to tell her he's sorry? She's involved somehow. But I don't know how."

He nodded. "Let's keep going."

We had another two hours of driving to Petunia's farm, and then we'd have to hike the rest of the way. We'd brought water, food, and other supplies, and kept our wristbands on. Hopefully, all would go well, and we'd either find Al or question Petunia and return before sundown, but I knew better than to count on that. So far, nothing had gone well with this whole investigation.

Ganja had lent me some of Angelica's clothes. They were more appropriate for a jungle trek, meaning they weren't see-through and covered me in a way that would hopefully keep me from getting scratched by prickly plants or stung by nasty insects. He'd stayed behind, waiting for news from Angelica's kidnappers. He was a mess. He felt so guilty. I understood that feeling well.

Before we took off on our excursion, I'd left Jax's diamond ring in the hotel safe. I didn't want to risk losing it in the jungle. Oddly enough, even though I'd only worn it a few days, my hand felt bare without it. Strange but true. He still wore his—even stranger.

I stopped looking at my hand and turned to Jax. "What's the story on Ganja Green? I know he was a smuggler and owns casinos, but everyone in the nature elf community adores him. Is he truly legit?"

"He is now," said Jax, his eyes on the road. "That wasn't always the case. It changed a few years ago when an accident occurred at one of his casinos. Someone died, and it shook Ganja to his core. He decided he wanted to change his life and his business, and he did."

"That's remarkable," I said. "Not everyone can change."

Jax must have heard something in my voice. "It's a matter of wanting it bad enough. Of realizing that the life you're living isn't truly your own and figuring out how to fix it. Or it can be finding the strength to walk away and not look back. People do change. It's not impossible."

I didn't know if we were still talking about Ganja or not. Jax seemed to speak from personal experience. I studied his profile, so handsome and strong, and wondered what exactly he'd had to walk away from. It must have been something significant.

I cleared my throat. "Maybe the best way to look at it is that we shouldn't assume we know the reasons behind someone's actions. They can be different from how they appear."

"And now you're thinking like a detective," he said, his face practically glowing with pride. "Well done."

I grinned at him, glad his sad moment had passed. "I learned from the best."

The road ended, so we came to a stop. Jax put the Jeep in park and turned to me. "This is where the fun begins. Are you sure you're ready for this?"

"Hiking through the rainforest? I'm a pro at this point, Jax."

"If you say so."

We got out of the Jeep and put on our backpacks. "Here goes nothing," I said.

He took my hand in his. "No, Tink. Here goes something. We're going to find Petunia's farm and solve this case."

I admired his optimism. I had my doubts.

Jax used a GPS device Reggie had given him. We knew the coordinates for Petunia's farm, and we knew it would be a hike, but we didn't realize how long it would take. Traveling on foot in the jungle was different, path or no path. We had a path to follow, but there were unforeseen obstacles. My unlucky streak continued.

Moments into our journey, the sky darkened, and rain began to fall. And fall. And fall. A thick curtain of rain went on for nearly an hour, drenching both of us and making the path muddy and slick.

"It's like ice skating," I said, sliding straight into Jax.

He managed to keep his footing. I lost my shoes several times, and we had to fight the mud and the suction it created to get them out.

"Maybe we should go back," he said, handing me my mud-covered shoe.

I shook my head. "Nope. It's all downhill from here. Literally. If we go back, we have to climb that muddy mountain. I'm not sure we can make it. Let's keep moving forward."

Jax didn't seem convinced. I doubted my own decision when we hit the base of the mountain and had to cross a rain-swollen creek.

"On the map, this creek looked much smaller," said Jax. "Are you sure you can do this?"

I gave him a thumbs up and my signature wink. Maybe I need to call it the "Tink Wink." It made sense.

"No problem," I said. "I've got this."

It turned out it was a problem. Jax made it over the creek with ease. I slipped on a moss-covered rock halfway through and fell into the water. The current carried me several hundred feet downstream before I grabbed a tree branch and pulled myself out. Jax burst through the bushes to find me lying on the bank, exhausted.

"Is it too late to change my mind? I want to go back to the spa. I want a watermelon daiquiri and a five-course meal and sex."

He nearly fell in the creek himself. "Sex?"

"I'm kidding," I said, pushing myself into a sitting position. "I wanted to see if you were paying attention. Honestly, I'm even too tired for sex right now."

He helped pull me to my feet. Thanks to the swim in the creek, at least I wasn't as muddy anymore. I twisted my hair to wring it out as Jax checked his GPS.

"We're close," he said. "Your little trip down the creek saved us some time."

"Hey, I'm always willing to help."

He pointed at an area downstream from where we stood. "If we follow the creek for half a mile, we should arrive at Petunia's farm."

"Awesome. Maybe we'll even make it before nightfall."

Wishful thinking on my part, but we made it there as the sun set. It was surprisingly easy to find. We just followed the sounds of music and laughter. Tiki lights burned, and a band played as people danced and sang. I smelled the aroma of meat being cooked over a fire and saw a long table laden with food. A tall man wearing nothing but a loin cloth and a colorful mask that covered half his face greeted us with a broad smile. His mask had feathers on it. His loin cloth had feathers, too. He looked like a giant, nearly naked, tropical bird, but at least he was friendly. He spoke to us like we belonged there.

"You made it! And it looks like you had quite the trip. Welcome."

Jax acted as confused as I felt. I shot him a look that conveyed we should roll with it as the man continued speaking. "I am Chrysanthemum Morifolium. Quite the mouthful, I know. Everyone calls me Mori."

"Hi, Mori," I said. "I'm Tink. This is my husband, Jax."

That lie slid off my tongue so easily now. It should have concerned me, but it didn't.

Mori grinned at us some more. He was high, but a happy kind of high. "Good to meet you, and welcome to the harvest festival. Petunia put me in charge of welcoming guests. You arrived in the nick of time. We only have one hut left. Follow me. I'll show you to your quarters. You can freshen up and join us for the meal. I bet you're starving. I keep telling Petunia to put in a real road, but she refuses. She likes things the way they are, I guess."

He showed us to a small, thatched hut. "The showers are in that building," he said, pointing to a wooden structure only a few yards away. "Costumes, if you choose to wear them, are inside the bathing lodge. Clothing is optional, of course. Most of us end up naked by the end of the night anyway. And the masks must stay on until midnight. That's the only rule."

He waved a cheery goodbye, and we watched him go. The loincloth only covered his front. The back was open for all the world to see.

"Well, this is interesting," said Jax.

"I'm too hungry and exhausted to try to figure it out now." I went into the hut and dropped my soggy backpack onto the floor. "First, we shower. Then we eat. Then we party. And at some point, we also find Al, bring him in for questioning, and solve the case, but the showering comes first."

"Agreed," said Jax, getting a towel for each of us. "And with any luck, they'll have watermelon daiquiris."

I grinned at him. "Now you're talking. Let's do this. We're so close. I can feel it."

He put a finger to my lips. "Shhh. Don't jinx it."

His reaction surprised me. "I never thought of you as the superstitious type."

"All dark elves are superstitious," he said, glancing around as we walked to the showers. "And something isn't quite right here. I feel it in my bones. Be alert, Tink. This isn't over yet. Not by a long shot."

TWENTY-TWO

It turned out Jax Grayson looked really terrific in a loin cloth. I didn't feel as spectacular in my bikini top and tiny mesh skirt with a G-string underneath, but Jax carried the look well enough for both of us. We put on our masks, similar to Mori's, and headed to the feast hand in hand.

Let me say, the nature elves know how to party. Most of the elves were naked, but we were used to that by now. The food was delicious, the drinks strong, and the music made everyone want to dance. A giant bonfire, lit in the center of the compound, burned brightly, flames leaping into the air.

Jax and I grabbed a plate of food and sat at one of the long tables set up for guests. The whole group was in a great mood, discussing the excellent harvest. Mori sat next to us, and he seemed to know everyone.

"Have you attended the harvest party before?" he asked, spearing a bite of succulent meat with his fork.

"First time," I said.

"You're in for a real treat. And we've had a great year." He waved a hand to indicate the tables laden with food.

"Everything here was grown locally. And we had more to export this year than ever before."

"What do you export?" asked Jax.

"Bananas. Papaya. Dragon fruit. Cabbage. A few other things." He gave us a wink. "Have you tried the dragon fruit mojito?"

He grabbed a pitcher and poured both of us a glass. "Wow. That's delicious," I said. "It's the best mojito I've ever tasted."

"I made it," he said proudly. "I love dragon fruit."

"You're a master," I said, and he grinned. "What happens next?"

"Petunia will give a little speech. And we'll all go to the Actun Tunichil Muknal— the Cave of the Crystal Sepulcher."

"Sepulcher?" asked Jax.

"Tomb. The bones of the Crystal Maiden are there—the skeleton of a young girl. A victim of a ritual sacrifice. The surface of the skeleton's bones sparkle. Humans say it's due to weathering, and to them it appears as if it's covered in fairy dust. They think it's 'magical,' and they aren't wrong. She wasn't a human. She was a Christmas elf. Like you, Tink."

It didn't strike me as odd that Mori recognized me as a Christmas elf. The differences between our races were evident from first sight. It did worry me initially that Mori welcomed us without question, but there were elves from all the tribes here tonight. Of course, the majority were nature elves, but I saw quite a few air elves, a bunch of water elves, several other Christmas elves, and even two other dark elves. The only elves missing from the party were snow elves, but that made sense. They couldn't handle the heat.

They were even less capable of handling the jungle than Christmas elves.

"They sacrificed Christmas elves?"

Mori shrugged. "All we know is that a Christmas elf died there centuries ago, and only her bones survived to tell the tale." He studied me closely. "Did you know that even your bones sparkle? Most people think it's your skin that has that quality. It goes much deeper. The Crystal Maiden is proof."

"Okay. Not creepy at all. Why are we going there exactly?"

"It's where the Wajxaqub' B'atz' ceremony will be performed. It happens every 260 days and celebrates a new cycle of the Mayan calendar. The histories of the Mayans and nature elves are intertwined, you see. It was that way for centuries. I mean, the veil was in place, but we worked around it if you know what I mean."

I had no idea what he meant. Jax didn't seem to either, but Mori kept talking. "Every year, someone is chosen to be the keeper of the calendar. It's a sacred duty. They'll act as a spiritual guide for our whole community. Petunia has been the keeper for years but is ready to step down. She'll intro- duce the new keeper tonight, and they'll start their duties immediately. That's why we have to be in the cave. Caves are portals, you see. They connect the sky, the earth, the sea, and the creatures of all the worlds, both elven and human. Can you both swim?" We nodded. "Good. You have to go through water to get into the cave."

"Water?"

"It's a sacred spring as well as a cave. You only have to swim a few feet. There are places inside that the water is knee deep, but you'll be fine." Mori got to his feet. "I have to help Petunia prepare. The unmasking will be at midnight in the cave. Enjoy the rest of your meal, but don't overeat. You'll need to climb through the cave to get to the tomb, and some of those openings are pretty narrow."

I sensed Jax stiffen next to me. After Mori left, I turned to him. I couldn't see much of his face, but he looked paler than usual.

"Are you okay?"

"I'm fine," he said. "I don't like caves."

"But you're a dark elf. You grew up in caves."

"Exactly."

Before I could question him further, a tiny woman climbed onto the wooden stage. She had on a dress woven in bright colors and a mask made of flowers and feathers. The crowd grew quiet, and she spoke.

"Welcome everyone, old friends and new. We're so happy you could join us for this sacred celebration. We have much to be thankful for, including wonderful crops, a thriving business, and many new connections. We plan for more success in the coming year, and I'm sure we'll have it under the guidance of our new calendar keeper."

The people cheered. The atmosphere felt like a combination of a Christmas celebration on the North Pole with a corporate sales event. Petunia went on about profit margins, exports, and farming methods.

"I didn't realize farming was such big business," I said softly to Jax.

"That depends entirely on what you're growing."

Even though half his face was covered with a mask, I knew him well enough to understand that he was on the verge of figuring something out. Something big. I wanted to ask him more, but Petunia announced it was time to head to the cave.

"Keep an eye out for Al," said Jax. "He might be here somewhere."

The festive crowd marched down a jungle path accompanied by the sound of drums and, oddly enough, an accordion. The drummers carried the barrel-shaped drums on their shoulders and sang a cheerful, uplifting song. I had no idea what the words meant, but it seemed happy. Another person had what appeared to be turtle shells hanging from his shoulder. He played the shells like a snare drum.

I couldn't stop myself from dancing along to the music. Jax held my hand, his expression alert. He was worried about something, but I couldn't ask him about it now. People surrounded us, and the music was loud. I would have had to shout to be heard.

I didn't see Al, although, with all the masks, it was hard to tell. Perhaps after the unmasking ceremony at midnight, we'd be better able to spot him.

The group stopped at a clearing in front of a giant cave. Water poured out in a gentle waterfall over rocks shaped like steps. The clearing was lit with tiki torches, but the mouth of the cave seemed dark and foreboding. Jax's grip tightened on my hand.

"Maybe we should turn around," he said, swallowing hard. He looked like he might get sick.

"No, we can't. I'll go inside. You stay here."

A fine sheen of sweat glistened on his body. He was terrified. "Are you sure?"

I nodded, kissing his cheek. Some of the older elves were staying behind in the clearing, as were a few pregnant elves and young elflings. "I'll be fine. What could go wrong?"

I'd wanted to make him laugh—no such luck. "Be careful. Stay with the group. Keep your wristband on. Do you have your phone?"

I held it up to him. "I do, but no reception."

"At least I can track it if you get lost."

"I won't get lost. I promise. I'll be back as soon as I can."

I waved at him over my shoulder as I followed the rest of the group into the cave's gaping mouth. Many of the elves carried flaming torches, which made it less scary. We first had to swim, as Mori had told us, but the water was surprisingly warm. Once we got through the cave entrance, the water was only knee-deep. That wasn't too bad, but we also had to climb rocks, squeeze through crevices, and work our way through a maze leading to the cave's sacred center.

Jax would never have made it. I had no idea he was claustrophobic until tonight. Oddly enough, it made me feel good that I could do something he couldn't.

The sight of the Crystal Maiden caused a strange stirring of sadness in my heart. Who was this Christmas elf, and how had she ended up here, deep in the belly of this dark cave? Her bones did, indeed, sparkle. And although I hung in the back of the group, I had a clear view. It nearly brought me to tears.

Petunia knelt next to the body of the long-dead elf and said a silent prayer, her eyes closed, and her head bowed. I was surprised to see tears running down her cheeks. The rest of the assembled elves were quiet, too. A few cried silently, and as Petunia knelt, the only sound was the dripping of water from the stalactites hanging down from the ceiling.

She got slowly to her feet, her eyes still on the skeleton. "Thank you for your sacrifice. May you rest here in peace forever and may our future sparkle as brightly as your sacred bones."

Someone began singing a sad and mournful song. Others joined in. I had no idea what it meant, but I felt it to the core of my sparkly little bones.

When the song ended, Petunia lifted her face and smiled. "It is time. I have been the calendar keeper for the last few decades, but it's time for a new elf to take my place. She will guide us, advise us, and lead us into a better and more prosperous future. Her mother, who died many years ago, was my close friend. I was happy to reunite with her and even happier when this wonderful and deserving elf agreed to take my place as keeper."

The crowd chuckled at her joke. I went on my tiptoes to see who might be taking Petunia's place. She gestured to someone in the group, and a woman stepped forward.

She was tall, with flowing dark hair and the sparkle every Christmas elf has to their skin. I concluded her father must have been a Christmas elf but couldn't figure out why this woman looked so familiar. Even her posture somehow rang a bell in my head.

The woman wasn't wearing much, only a tiny string bikini. Most of her bottom was bare. It wasn't until she stepped closer to the skeleton and embraced Petunia in a warm hug that things started to come together for me.

I was staring at her butt, wondering how it could be that perky, when I realized the pale skin of her derriere was also decorated—with a rose tattoo.

Excellent posture. Long, dark hair. Graceful. Beautiful. Rose tattoo.

"Greetings, everyone," she said, a smile on her perfect lips, and that was the final confirmation. I knew who she was, and that realization made me panic. I slipped and nearly fell. The elf next to me grabbed my arm.

"Are you okay?" she asked.

"Yes," I said. "I need some air. It feels a bit close in here."

"That happens. You can leave through that opening. The way is well lit," she said, her eyes concerned. "But stay on the path. If you get lost in here, they'll never find out. Look what happened to that poor elf." She tilted her head to indicate the skeleton.

"Good point. I'll be careful. Thanks."

As she recommended, I sped out of the cave, sticking to the illuminated path. I fell only once, scraping my hands and bottom on a rock, but I made it to the cave entrance with relative ease.

I saw Jax pacing back and forth as I swam outside. As soon as he saw me, he rushed over, splashing through the shallow water.

"What happened?" He noticed my scraped hands. "Are you hurt?"

Shaking my head, I led him to the side of the pool. I started shivering, but it wasn't from the cold.

"The woman in the cave," I said. "The new keeper. I recognized her. I mean, I recognized her butt."

He put his hands on my cheeks and stared at me. "What are you talking about, Tink?"

"The new keeper. She had a rose tattoo. She was there the night Scarlet died. She was the fourth dancer. But it gets worse."

"What are you saying?"

"The woman with the rose tattoo is Angelica Frost."

TWENTY-THREE

We raced back on the jungle path toward Petunia's compound. We hoped to get to an area with cell phone reception, but no such luck.

"What should we do?" I asked, taking off my mask. The others were still at the cave, and the compound was empty.

Jax rubbed his chin with the back of his hand. He'd taken off his mask as well. "We can't leave. Not in the middle of the night. We'll have to set off at daybreak. Hopefully, everyone will still be asleep, and we can slip out unnoticed."

I checked my phone. Still no service.

"It's eleven o'clock," I said. "The unmasking is at midnight. That means we're alone here for an hour. Should we look around?"

"We should," said Jax. "Because none of this is adding up."

As we walked around the compound, we discussed the case. "Angelica must have killed Scarlet. Why? Was she trying to kill Ganja?"

"If Angelica was the murderer, I doubt she was trying to kill Ganja."

"What do you mean?"

"Well, she could have killed him at any time while at the resort. They were sleeping together. Hanging out together. Eating together."

I covered my mouth with my hand. "Do you think Angelica is the one that messed with our honeymoon cake? She went to the restroom before they brought it out. She was gone an abnormally long time for lipstick."

"That's possible, but why?"

"I don't know. She's always hated me, but she seemed so nice as we were on our way to the meditation session. Not her normal self at all."

"Do you think it was all an act?"

"Maybe. Angelica was truly evil when we were in high school. Both you and Ganja said that people change, but I had my doubts." I winced. "We have to tell Ganja she wasn't kidnapped. She must have set the whole thing up."

"Exactly, and that means several things."

"Yeah, I know what it means," I said, biting my lip. "It means I'm the worst detective ever. I stood right next to Angelica and didn't recognize her. I don't deserve to be in the EBI. Director Finn was right, and Noelle was right, too. I set up that whole undercover operation to prove I could do it. There was nothing professional about it. I'm a failure and a fraud, and everything others say about me is right. The first case I helped you crack was a fluke. I'm a one-hit wonder, a dud, and I'm done. I'm out. I'm resigning as soon as we get back to the North Pole."

He studied my face, his expression unreadable. "I never thought of you as a quitter."

I let out a bitter laugh. "There is grace in giving up

when you know you can't do the job. I'm being honest. Give me some credit."

"No," he said, his face dark with fury. "I will not give you any credit. Not when you're refusing to do the same for yourself."

He looked so hot when he was all angry and sweaty and partially naked that I forgot to feel bad for myself for a second and enjoyed the sight of his heaving bare chest. When I realized he awaited some sort of response, I did—in my usual intelligent way.

"Huh?"

He came a step closer until we were almost nose to nose. "Did you not go into a cave when I couldn't?"

"Yeah, but—"

"And have you not saved my life and others on several occasions?"

"Well, yes—"

"And did you not figure out that Angelica was at the crime scene?"

He ran a hand through his dark hair. The action made his bicep bulge. It was challenging for me to hold a serious conversation with a nearly naked Jax.

"I guess...?"

He put his hands on my shoulders. "There is no guessing. Are you experienced? No. Have you been at this long? No. Are you far too brave and impulsive for your own good? Yes. Are you quite mad? Definitely."

"Hey—"

"But are you a good detective?" He paused, his gaze locked on mine. "The answer is a resounding yes. There is no doubt in my mind that you will be an excellent agent one day. You're the most naturally gifted investigator I've ever had the pleasure of knowing. And you're also one of the smartest and most intuitive people I've ever met."

"I am?"

"You are." He took a step back, as if our near nakedness and proximity were difficult for him too. "And what do those instincts say we should do now?"

I considered the question. "Find Al, if we can. Figure out what exactly Petunia is exporting that gives her such a great profit margin. Let Ganja know Angelica is a lying sack of—"

"Tinklebelle Holly?"

Jax and I both turned in surprise to see a woman approach with a young girl. The woman was masked, but I knew who she was right away. "Lily?"

They still had their masks on, but I could tell it was Lily by the purple hair. "What are you two doing here?" she asked. "And with no masks?"

"Oh. We got lost. I wasn't feeling great." I lowered my voice and made a gesture to indicate downing drinks. "Mori's mojitos got me."

"Well, I'm glad I caught you. I want to introduce you to my daughter. Holly, this is the woman I named you after. The woman who saved my life."

Holly tugged on her purple pigtail. "Nice to meet you," she said.

"And this is my husband, Jax," I said. Now I was lying to children. Great. But my little namesake bought it.

"Nice to meet you, Mr. Jax," said Holly.

To my surprise, Jax lowered himself until he was at eye level with her. "Nice to meet you, too. Did you have fun at the party?"

She nodded. "I did, but I don't like caves. That's why Mommy brought me back here."

Jax gazed at her solemnly. "I'm the same. I hate caves. Which is terrible news since I'm a dark elf, and dark elves live in caves."

Holly giggled. "You're silly."

Lily smiled at her daughter. "And you're sleepy. Time for bed, little one." She turned to us. "Nice seeing the two of you. I'm glad you could make it to the party. But you'd better put your masks back on. The rules here are pretty lax, but they take the masks seriously."

"Got it," I said, putting the mask back on my face. Jax did the same.

"And Tink, one more thing. It's an old nature elf saying. *Wen cak-roach mek dance, e' no invite fowl.*"

I ATTEMPTED to translate it and failed. "All I caught was something about cockroaches...?"

Lily leaned closer. "When the cockroach makes a dance, he doesn't invite the fowl. It means don't look for trouble, my friend. If you do, you're sure to find it."

After they left, I shot Jax a worried look. "Did Lily tell us to stop snooping in an adorable yet colorful way?"

"Indeed, she did. And you know what that means, right?"

"That someone is hiding something, and we need to figure out what it is."

"Exactly."

He grinned, the effect disarming me as it always did. Would I ever get used to how the usually serious Jax Grayson looked when he smiled? I doubted it. I tried to contain my racing heart and focus.

"Where do we start?"

He pointed to a door on a long, wooden building marked Do Not Enter. "How about there?"

"Sounds like a plan."

The first building we inspected held lodging facilities for farm workers. The second building contained equipment, like tractors and plows. The third building, the one furthest from the compound's center, had something else inside.

"Is this a lab?" I asked, taking off my mask and setting it down. Jax did the same.

"I believe the term is 'kitchen' since they are cooking something."

Long metal tables, covered with beakers, Bunsen burners, and mixers, sat under low-hanging lights. A series of high windows were cracked open, allowing a soft breeze to enter the room.

"The windows are high so that no one can look inside and see what's in here," said Jax. "I think we can guess what they're producing."

"Rock candy?"

"Bingo. We'd better be careful. We don't want to alert anyone to our presence."

We turned off the overhead lights and used the flashlights on our phones. The place smelled like a mix of chemicals and kerosene. Boxes of baking soda stood against one wall.

"Why do they have so much baking soda?" I asked.

"Rock candy is made by boiling a mix of powdered candicocane, water, and sodium bicarbonate," he said. "Which is baking soda. They use it to remove the hydrochloride. That creates a solid substance that can be broken up into rocks." He pointed to other items on the table. "The dangerous part is that they're cutting it with other agents. In this case, it's likely telazol."

"Reindeer tranquilizer. But why?"

"To increase both the quantity of the drug and the effect. It's all about profits and the bottom line. And Petunia is running quite the operation here." He picked up some leaves in a basket. "These are coca leaves. I guarantee she grows them on her farm. That's why this place is so remote and hard to access. But I bet they have straight routes to get the drugs out. She must be using the breach in the veil. The question is, how?"

Jax gathered some of the leaves and samples from the table. Since he had on nothing but a loincloth, and I didn't have pockets in my mesh skirt or the G-string beneath it, I looked around for something to carry the samples. I found boxes against one wall. They were marked *Fragilee*.

I snorted. "They spelled fragile wrong."

The boxes were too big to carry, but inside were small, white plastic pouches. They looked like cooling gel packages to keep food cool when shipping, except they were empty. Next to the pile of boxes was a squeeze bottle of clear gel. I picked up one of the empty freezer bags, planning to give it to Jax to carry his samples, and that's when I noticed several bags on another table that had been filled and sealed.

"Jax, why would they be filling gel cooling pouches in a rock candy kitchen?"

It didn't make sense. Jax came over to check it out with a confused frown. "I have no idea."

I bit my lip as I tried to put the pieces together. "Petunia legitimately exports fruits and vegetables. She ships them all over the elven world."

"She does."

I picked up one of the filled cooling bags. "These things are cheap to buy. Why is Petunia filling them herself?"

I studied the bag. It looked like a regular gel pack for cooling. It wasn't until I kneaded the contents that I got a surprise.

"Here," I said, handing it to Jax. "Feel this."

He did, and his eyes widened in shock. "There is something hard inside. It feels like..."

"Rocks?"

"Yes." He gave me another one of those heart-stopping grins. "You did it, Tink. You figured it out. This is how they're distributing the drugs. When the packs are frozen, you can't feel the rocks. But boiling it down to rock form, freezing it, and thawing it increases the potency. Most drug dealers wouldn't do that since repeat customers are their goal, but these guys don't seem to care. They're changing the chemical composition. They created a super drug. And if this gets into the human world, it'll be an even greater disaster."

The idea that they were killing elves for a profit and that they were aware they were doing it made me sick. "Do you think Angelica knows?"

Jax snorted. "I would think she does. They made her the keeper, right?"

I nodded. "And Petunia was the previous keeper, but it looks like Angelica is now in charge of this operation. By the way, when I was in the cave with the Christmas elf skeleton, I also discovered Angelica's birth mother was a nature elf and close friends with Petunia."

The circle was getting tighter and tighter, but I still had questions. Jax seemed to have some as well.

"So Angelica possibly killed Scarlet?" he asked. "But why?"

"I don't know. I also don't see how Al fits into this whole mess, and I don't understand Ganja's role."

He shrugged. "Ganja has money. And, as a former smuggler, he has channels Petunia may not have tapped into before. Other ways to distribute her product. It's all about profits."

"But do you think Ganja knew?"

"I doubt it. He didn't lie when he said he's been a legitimate businessman for years."

"You told me there was an accident at one of his casinos."

"Yes. He told me a little about it while we were hanging out in the mineral springs. A kid celebrating his 21st birthday got wasted and thought he could fly. He jumped off the roof of the casino and died. He was a good kid from a good family, and Ganja took it hard. Charges were filed against Ganja, but they didn't stick. The judge ruled Ganja couldn't be held responsible for the other elf's decisions or actions, but Ganja felt responsible. He cleaned up his act, set rules about not overserving customers, and even made his rooftops inaccessible. He saw the kid die that night, and it changed him."

"For the better."

"For the better. And that's why I don't think Ganja knows about any of this. If he did, he'd be the first to shut it down."

"But he's in love with Angelica, and love can make us do crazy things."

"Well, that's true." Jax gave me a wry smile. I wasn't sure what he meant by that, but he continued talking. "I don't think Ganja is in love with Angelica. He likes her, feels responsible for her, and enjoys having a beautiful woman on his arm. He's also a little obsessed with the society pages."

"Oh, yes. *Elf* magazine."

"But do I think he has some sort of undying love for Angelica? They've only been together a few months. That isn't enough time."

I glanced at my phone. It was a few minutes after midnight. "Speaking of time, we need to get out of here. The others will be back soon."

We gathered the samples, put them into empty gel packs, and were about to slip outside when the lights went on inside the building. We blinked, our eyes adjusting, but what I saw made my breath catch in my throat.

Petunia, Mori, Angelica, and the rest of the gang stood in front of us, unmasked and furious. Angelica glared at me, the expression on her face reminiscent of her high school bullying days.

"Stinky Tinky. We meet again."

There was no point in denying why we were here. "I knew you hadn't changed. I wanted to give you the benefit of the doubt, but I knew you were still rotten. I didn't think you'd end up being a murderer, though."

She snorted. "Murderer? Seriously? Ew. You must be the worst detectives ever. I didn't kill anyone."

I studied her face. I knew Angelica well enough to get a sense of when she lied. To my surprise, she seemed to be telling the truth.

Jax must have sensed it, too. "But who killed Scarlet, and why were you in the club that night?" he asked.

She let out a huff. "You're cute, but your questions are boring. I'll answer them, though, since you are both screwed." She ticked off her fingers. "One. I have no idea who killed Scarlet, but I think Ganja does. Two. I was at the club to get something that belonged to Petunia."

I blinked in surprise. "You were there to get the flash drive."

"Bingo. Wow, Tink. You're super smart."

Jax turned to Petunia. "Your son wasn't working for you?"

Petunia bristled. "My son the traitor? He got the flash drive from my former scumbag accountant. They were working together."

"Red," I said with a gasp. "Scarlet's brother."

"Exactly. He blamed me for Ruby's death, which is a joke. It's like what they say, rock candy doesn't kill people. Taking too much of it kills people. It's not my fault Al's girl was a druggie."

"But she wasn't a druggie. Scarlet said Ruby had never used drugs before. She barely even drank."

Petunia rolled her eyes. "Like she would know. Does a mother ever truly know her child? I mean, look at my half-wit son. He gave Scarlet the flash dive with all my records on it."

"Why?" I asked.

Petunia lifted her hands as if confused. "After Ruby died, Al called to let me know he planned to give up his own mother. He wanted to go on the straight and narrow—what a laugh. Ruby was a weakling. I didn't get her hooked on the drugs. I didn't make her take them. Yes, I made them, but it's about personal choice."

It sounded like a shaky argument to me. "That flash drive must be pretty important."

"Scarlet thought so," said Petunia. "And Scarlet was no dummy. I knew we had to stop her. She went a little crazy after her daughter died. She made a lot of threats. She suspected I might be involved. The flash drive would have proved it, so Angelica went to the club to get it back. She didn't have to, though. She brought her boyfriend with her as a backup in case something went wrong. He had no idea what was going on, but we got lucky. It ended up that Ganja got it for her."

"We love Gan-Gan," said Angelica. "And he's so trusting for a gangster. He thought he was coming to see me dance. I told him it turned me on. But do you know what really turns me on? All of Ganja's...assets."

I felt terrible for Ganja, Scarlet, Al, and anyone else who had contact with these women. "What's on that flash drive?" I asked.

"Accounting stuff," said Angelica. "Scarlet was always interested in the accounting stuff, but I'm getting bored. Why are you still talking?"

I had flashbacks to my high school days, but there were other things I needed to know. "Did you truly care about Ganja, or was that an act?"

She seemed genuinely surprised by my question. "Of course, I care about him. He's hot, rich, and dirty enough to be appealing. Also, he has connections. Even if he isn't using them anymore, being close to him allows me to tap into his system. Those glitches in the veil? They aren't glitches at all. They're doorways to a whole new group of customers. Humans."

"Wow. You're good at this, Angelica," said Jax. "I never pegged you for a criminal mastermind, but you know what you're doing."

She shrugged. "I majored in marketing. I'm kind of a genius. I'm also highly skilled at branding. That's how I convinced Ganja I was into volunteering and all that crap. As if. I hate poor elves. They smell funny."

"Clever girl," said Petunia. "And Ganja Green also has a conscience. You used that in your favor as well."

"I did," said Angelica, beaming. "I needed to get away so I could come here for the ceremony. It worked out perfectly when Ganja freaked out and thought I was kidnapped. While he was looking for me, I returned to our room, grabbed the flash drive, and left a ransom note. Why not make a little cash from the deal?"

"You truly are a terrible person, Angelica."

"Whatever. Let's finish this. I want to get back to the party."

Mori shifted nervously from one foot to another. "But what are we going to do with them, boss?"

He looked at Petunia as he spoke. She pointed at Angelica. "She's the boss now, Mori. Let her decide."

Angelica's pretty face hardened, making her look nearly repulsive. "They're EBI agents," she said. "We need to get rid of them."

Mori looked like he might throw up. "Oh, no. We can't kill EBI agents. That would bring everyone from Elf Central down on our heads. I mean, we have people inside, but they wouldn't be able to stop it if two agents ended up murdered. And Frank Yummy—"

"Stop talking, Mori," said Angelica, her gaze as cold as the ice on the North Pole. "We aren't going to murder anyone. I know exactly what to do."

TWENTY-FOUR

Angelica's big plan was to knock us out and drop us into a dark, scary place with no water, no food, and no cell phones. It was cold there, too.

I opened my eyes, feeling sick and queasy. I vaguely remembered someone placing a cloth over my mouth that smelled funny, but nothing after that. I felt bruised and battered, and my ankle hurt. A sharp stab of pain hit me when I tried to move it, causing me to gasp. Jax sat next to me, still in his loincloth. He cradled his arm close to his chest.

"Are you hurt?"

"My ankle," I said. "It might be broken. How about you?"

"My arm," he said. "And I may have a cracked rib. Or two."

"What happened?" My voice sounded scratchy and strange and echoed off the stone walls surrounding us.

"Well, they drugged us with telazol."

"Why is it always reindeer tranquilizer?" I asked. "Does no one use chloroform anymore?"

He chuckled and winced as if laughing caused him pain. "Good point. But I have to imagine it was a matter of convenience. They cut the rock candy with telazol, so it was handy."

"And strong."

"That too."

I'd spent some time working at the reindeer paddock on the North Pole. Some of the reindeer were jerks, namely Comet, but most were nice. We'd used telazol on them frequently, and now that I knew what it felt like, it made me sympathetic for the reindeer.

"Where are we?" I asked, sitting up straighter.

"I believe it's some sort of well," said Jax, his voice tight and strange. "After they drugged us, they dropped us in here. We're both lucky to be alive. The Mayans used natural wells, known as 'cenotes,' to sacrifice victims to the gods. They believed that the god of rain and water lived here. I think we're in one of those cenotes right now."

I touched the wall. It was cold, damp stone. "Wow. It sucks to be us."

"It certainly does."

I felt for my tracking wristband. "They took my wristband. Do you have yours?"

He shook his head. "Nope."

The only light came from the moon, which was full. Otherwise, the well was deep, dark, and terrifying—especially for Jax.

"Are you okay?"

"Not really."

"Can you tell me about it?"

He sighed. "When I was small, my father used to leave me alone in dark caves. Sometimes, he did it as a punishment. Other times, I believe he simply found it entertaining.

Dark elves think it builds character for a child to find their way home after being abandoned. It's a rite of passage." He glanced up at the moon so far above us. "But once there was a rockslide, and I was trapped alone in the dark for three days."

My heart went out to him. "How old were you?"

"Eight. Fortunately, I had water in the cave. It came from a small spring. But there was no light at all. I'd grown up underground, but that cave was different. Small. Dark. Damp. And I was terrified I might never get out, but also scared about what my father might say if I did get out. He did not approve of weakness or failure of any kind. And even though I hadn't caused the rockslide, I wasn't clever enough to avoid it either."

"Wow. He makes Grandma Gingersnap sound like a cupcake," I said, gently wrapping my arms around him. This was the most he'd ever said to me about his family. He leaned into me for comfort.

"Grandma Gingersnap is a cupcake," he said.

"You only say that because she adores you. And after learning more than I ever cared to about her dating history, I have to assume she has a thing for dark elves. It must run in the family."

"I guess a fondness for Christmas elves runs in my family, too.

Zakar of Neslos was my grandfather's brother."

I sat up straighter, squinting in the darkness to try to make out his features. "You're kidding."

He shook his head. "No, I'm not. But Uncle Zak was always a bit of a rebel. My father used to insult me by saying I was like him. I took it as a compliment." He glanced around. "My father would have a lot to say about our current predicament too."

The well's walls were steep, and the small circular entrance was at least fifteen feet above our heads. We sat in a few inches of water, with sharp rocks poking my bottom. My hands felt raw. My whole body felt raw, but I refused to complain. I had to stay strong. Jax needed me.

He had his face tucked into the curve of my neck. I kissed the top of his head. "We'll figure this out. It's going to be alright."

"Will we?" he asked, his voice muffled by my hair. He leaned back so that he could look at my face. "It's looking pretty hopeless. If we don't make it out of here, there is something I need you to know—"

I put my finger to his lips. "Tell me later because we are getting out of here, Jax. I promise you. And a Holly always keeps their promise."

He nodded, swallowing hard. "Okay. I believe you."

I squeezed his hand. "Let's look around and figure out what we're dealing with. Can you help me to my feet?"

It took a few tries, but we got up. I balanced precariously on one leg. My ankle was definitely broken. I'd lost my shoes, and the rocks at the bottom of the well jabbed at my skin. Jax had not only fractured his arm and hurt his ribs. He seemed to have dislocated his shoulder as well, on the same side as his broken bone. I remembered reading something about how dangerous and painful a dislocated shoulder could be, but Jax powered through. We felt our way around the sides of the well, looking for any way to escape. We couldn't find anything. No tunnels to crawl through. No ropes to grab onto. No handholds or steps to use to climb out. We were well and truly trapped.

Discouraged, we sank back down into the muck to rest. Something jabbed my back, and when I pulled it out, I realized it was some long-dead person's shin bone.

"Oh, holy night," I said, tossing it away. "We're screwed."

"Yep," said Jax.

"I mean really screwed."

"We are…"

A screeching sound came from above. I frowned. I recognized that screech. "Felix?"

Felix the howler monkey peeked over the edge of the well. I'd never been so happy to see a primate in my life.

"Hey, little buddy. Can you get us some help? Go tell Reggie we're trapped in a well."

"Did you seriously ask a howler monkey to—"

"Shhh," I said. "He's got something."

Felix lifted something over his head and threw it down into the well. It barely missed my head. I picked it up.

"Is that a flashlight?" asked Jax. "Clever little monkey."

Felix tossed something else down as well. "And one of my bras," I said, lifting it with one finger. "Gee. Thanks."

But Felix wasn't done yet. He tossed something else down. It landed on my shoulder, and I gagged as I brushed it off. "Monkey poo? Really? Can you do something useful and get help?"

Felix let out another screech, apparently annoyed that I hadn't appreciated his parting gift, and took off. I turned to Jax. "I'm sorry, Jax."

"Don't be sorry. At least we have the flashlight."

He turned it on, and the light nearly blinded us. Once my eyes adjusted, I studied him, and I could tell from the lines on his face how much he was hurting.

"We're in bad shape, Jaxy."

He reached for me with his good hand. "We are. But if I had to choose someone to die in a Mayan sacrificial well with, it would be you, Tink."

"Ditto." I let out a sigh. "And at least we have light now."

"We do."

"Noelle will feel so bad that she didn't accept my apology."

Jax chuckled. "Chief Sleigh will build a glittering monument in your honor."

I snorted. "Grandma Gingersnap will sign all the thank you cards for funeral flowers with FML Gingersnap."

He laughed and also cringed. "Ouch. Don't make me laugh. Please. What did you tell her FML meant?"

"Forever My Love. I told her it's how everyone signs cards now. It makes no sense at all, but she bought it. I have no idea why she continues to trust me for pop culture and social media advice. I obviously don't have her best interests at heart." I had to keep cracking jokes, or even thinking about my family would make me lose it. I turned to Jax. "What about you? How will your family react?"

He gave me a sad smile. "I don't know. I haven't spoken to any of them in years. Not since I betrayed them by taking a job at Elf Central and working for the Elven High Council."

"Why was that a betrayal?"

"Because I had certain responsibilities at home. I still hear from my mother. Not my father."

He grew silent. I felt so bad for him. And because I hated awkward silences, I jumped in to fill the void. "But do you know who is going to be devastated? Director O'Reilly. He will feel so sorry about how he spoke to us."

"Indeed. Maybe he'll even award us a posthumous medal of honor or something."

"That would be nice." I snuggled closer to him. "So, since we have nothing else to do to occupy what time we have left, let's talk about the case we almost solved. Who do you think killed Scarlet?"

"I don't know. We should go over the facts. We know it was not the evil Angelica."

"Yep. And may I say her name is false advertising. Everyone I know, Angel, Angelica, Angela, or Angelique, is a narcissist and rotten to their core."

"I don't know anyone with those names, but I believe you. Back to the murder, I'm certain whoever it was wanted to kill Ganja, not Scarlet."

"I agree. And I also think it was the same person who killed poor Gus Gravy."

"Yes, but how did they do it? Gus Gravy was stabbed. That's simple. But Scarlet's death is more complicated. What kind of weapon can kill someone and disappear like it never existed?"

I considered it. "That's the big question. We're still missing some connections. And I'm starting to think Scarlet was right about Ruby's death, too. Also, why did Mori mention Frank Yummy? Who was Al waiting for at the spa? And why did Angelica poison our honeymoon cake? It had to be her."

"I'm not sure. Perhaps she wanted to get rid of you? Perhaps you were a complication? I don't know, but at least we figured out the drug smuggling bit."

I gave him a thumbs up. "Yay for us. I wish we could put Petunia and her associates in jail. Especially Angelica-freaking-Frost. I think that might be what I most regret about dying here. Well, that and the other thing."

"What other thing?" he asked, his voice rough with exhaustion and pain.

I yawned, pressing my cheek against his uninjured shoulder. "Not sleeping with you."

He kissed the top of my head. "Trust me, Tink. I regret that, too. FML."

"FML, Jax." I turned to gaze up at him. "Wait. Do you mean it the original way or the Grandma Gingersnap way?"

He grinned at me, and even though we were doomed and in pain and about to die, it still made my heart beat faster. "Both," he said. "How about you?"

"Ditto."

It was the closest we'd get to a declaration of love, but it felt perfect. Whether we had moments together or years, Jax made me happy. Perhaps because death was so close, I saw things more clearly now, and despite our current predicament, I experienced something surprising. Something close to a miracle.

A moment of pure and unexpected joy. Right when we needed it most.

MY EYELIDS GREW HEAVY, and I must have dozed off. I had crazy, feverish dreams of being chased through the jungle by a creature with sharp claws and big teeth. I woke to a bright light shining directly into my face with a shadowy figure behind it.

"Crap on a cracker. Am I dead?"

The shadowy figure laughed and leaned closer. It was Ganja. "Not yet," he said, "but you're both pretty banged up."

It took me five seconds to realize this was not part of my dream. I sat up quickly, checking on Jax. Ganja had come to save us, and he'd brought help, namely Reggie and several others from the hotel staff. A person from the medical team was assessing Jax's injuries. Jax gave me a weary grin.

"We made it," he said.

I leaned closer and kissed him. "We did."

"You'll have time for all that honeymoon stuff later," said Ganja. "We need to get both of you to the hospital."

"How did you find us?" asked Jax.

"Well, Reggie is an excellent tracker—" he began, grinning. Reggie interrupted him.

"I am an excellent tracker, but that's not how we found you," he said. "I'm dating Lily Garland. She found out what had happened and called me. She had a satellite phone in her Jeep."

"Are Lily and Holly okay? Did they get out of there?"

He nodded. "They are back at the resort, safe and sound."

"Thank goodness. I need to thank her. I owe her one."

"From what I understand, this was a debt Lily was happy to repay. But that wasn't the only clue."

"What do you mean?" I asked.

"Well, your flashlight helped."

"That was Felix," I said. "He tossed it to us."

"The monkey?"

"Yes. He also threw poo at me. And my bra. I'm not sure what to read into that part."

"Maybe just let it go. Some things aren't meant to be understood. But the light helped us find you. As did this."

Ganja held up his phone, showing me a text from an unknown number. It consisted of two words—Altun Ha.

"We're at Altun Ha?" I frowned at him. "How?"

"They must have brought you through the breach. It's an old smuggling trick."

"But who sent you that message?"

Ganja put his phone back in his pocket. "I suspect it may have been Al Winkle. He owed me something. I guess that debt is now paid." Ganja hesitated, as if weighing his words. "Or it may have been someone else. Someone with a vested interest in keeping you and Jax alive. There is a great deal going on here, and a lot I don't understand, but I'm planning to figure it out."

"You and me both."

Hearing noise coming from above, I looked up. The sky had lightened, signifying it must be early morning, and I heard the sound of a helicopter in the distance. It seemed like quite the party had assembled on the surface. They sent down a portable rescue stretcher using ropes. I insisted they take Jax first. He was in much worse shape than me. Ganja stayed with me, and as they began lifting Jax, I touched Ganja's arm. There was a lot I had to tell him.

"I still have your coat. I need to get it back to you, but there is still blood and glitter on it. I want to have it dry cleaned first. And maybe exorcised."

He snorted. "The coat is the least of my concerns."

"Angelica wasn't kidnapped." I couldn't think of a way to soften the blow, so I simply blurted out the words.

"I figured as much," he said, his voice resigned. "When the flash drive went missing, I assumed it was her. I put it into the safe right in front of her. She watched me enter the combination. It was sort of a test of loyalty, I guess. She failed. Obviously."

"She's also one of the drug smugglers," I said. "The rock candy that killed Ruby came from Petunia's farm. They've been shipping it in boxes of produce, and, as of last night, Angelica is in charge of the whole operation."

Ganja let out a sigh. "That I did not know," he said. "But it doesn't surprise me. She does have a degree in marketing."

He wiggled his eyebrows, making me laugh. "Yes, I've heard that, too. But you cared about her."

"I did, but the better I got to know Angelica, the more I realized you were right."

"You did?"

"Yes, I did. She's a rotten apple. Bad at her core. And if the bad apple isn't removed, the whole barrel will spoil."

"Um, Ganja. You aren't planning to do anything illegal or unethical, are you?"

He seemed genuinely surprised. "No, but I will ensure they get what they deserve."

The rescue stretcher came back down. Ganja and Reggie gently lifted me onto it. I grabbed Ganja's sleeve. "And what exactly do they deserve? Ganja?"

"Justice," he said. "Nothing more, and nothing less."

TWENTY-FIVE

The helicopter ride to the hospital was short. Jax held my hand the whole time. It turned out I needed surgery on my ankle. Falling into the well caused me to break a bone and tear a tendon. After deciding it would be better for me to have that surgery at the North Pole, Jax and Ganja arranged a private jet to fly both of us back home. Ganja stayed behind to "tie up some loose ends." I didn't want to know what he meant by that, but I trusted him. Ganja, even though he'd made some poor choices in his life, was a good guy.

"I need to disappear for a bit. Be careful who you trust," he said, lowering himself so that he was even with me as I sat on my wheelchair on the tarmac. "Things are not always as they seem."

"Can you elaborate a little?"

He shook his head. "No, but everyone is a suspect. Remember that and stay close to Jax."

"Because he'll keep me safe?" I asked, a little annoyed.

"No. Because you'll keep each other safe."

He turned to leave. I stopped him. "I never got to thank Lily," I said. "She saved us."

"And you saved her," said Ganja. "Now you're even. There is always a score that must be settled, whether we like it or not. As we say in Belize, sleep wit' yo' own eye."

"That's as bad as the cockroach one. What does it mean?"

"Only rely on what you know. Not what others tell you."

I had one more question. "Who tried to kill you, Ganja? Who murdered Scarlet?"

He paused, emotions crossing over his features as he decided how to answer me. He came closer and lowered his voice so only I could hear.

"It's someone with a grudge. They have a score to settle, but the less you know, the better it will be for you." He kissed me softly on the cheek. "Goodbye, Tink. Take care of yourself. We'll meet again in better days."

And with that, he was off, and the medical team loaded me onto the plane. That part wasn't fun since I was in a temporary cast and miserable, but they got me set up nicely and propped my ankle up on pillows. I felt comfortably numb from the drugs I'd been given and incredibly happy to be alive.

Jax had a cast on his wrist. They'd popped his shoulder back into place at the emergency room. It hadn't been pleasant to watch, but he seemed relatively fine besides two broken bones in his wrist and the sore ribs. We'd both been given a lot of painkillers, and narcotics always made me feel like opening up and sharing all my feelings.

"You know, we said a lot of stuff when we were stuck in that well," I said.

"We did."

"Did you mean it?"

He took my hand and kissed it. "I did."

"All of it?"

"Yes, Tink."

"Even that part about regrets?"

"Of course."

"I have a suggestion for you." I wiggled my eyebrows and tilted my head to indicate the toilet. "Mile high club?"

He nearly choked on his drink. "I don't think that's a good idea," he said once he stopped coughing. "You're injured, and—"

I patted his hand. "I'm joking. I love being able to shock you. You're so easily shockable. But regarding the regrets thing, can we have a rain date?"

He lifted my hand and brought it to his lips. "We can. You know what they say about dark elves, don't you?"

"You're incredible in bed?"

He tossed back his head and laughed. "Well, besides that." When I didn't respond, he answered for me. "Like the Hollys, we always keep our promises."

"What about the job thing? And being professional?"

"I'm quitting," he said. "I made my decision when I was in that well. They offered me a diplomatic position on the Elven High Council a few months ago. I'd have to spend more time at Elf Central, but it might work."

"You've thought this out, haven't you?"

"I have. We can't go on like this. I might die of sexual frustration, and you could explode into a cloud of glitter and rainbows or something."

"A nice visual, but we can't have that, can we?"

"No, we can't."

I grabbed him as hard as possible without hurting him and kissed him. I couldn't stop kissing him. I would have taken Jax into that restroom if it weren't for our injuries. But I was in a happy, loopy fog as we landed on the North Pole. I couldn't put any weight on my foot, and crutches were challenging. Jax only had one usable arm, so Topper and a few team members came inside the plane to help. When Topper saw my green face, he lifted his eyebrows but didn't comment. My uncle, who waited for us inside the airport, stayed silent, too. Grandma Gingersnap, however, had no such reservations. Despite my cast and the wheelchair, she zeroed in on that first.

"Why are you still that horrible color?" she asked, leaning closer to get a better look. "You look like pond scum."

"That's because I am pond scum. Hi, Grandma. How are you? Any questions about anything else besides my coloring?"

She narrowed her eyes at me. "Do you seriously want me to start on how you nearly died? Again?"

"Yeah, maybe we should stick to my face. The woman at the spa said it'll take a few days. I think it's getting better."

"Agreed," said Jax. "And at least you don't have spots anymore."

"Thank you for bringing her back alive," she said, pulling Jax into a hug as she burst into tears. "I don't know what I'd do if I ever lost her."

She leaned against him, sobbing. Jax took it like a champ. He wrapped her in a hug with his good arm. "She's going to be fine," he said.

My uncle agreed with him. "Yes, Tink is a strong woman. And after her surgery, she'll be on crutches for quite some time. You'll have months of not having to worry about her. How much trouble can she get into while on crutches?"

Grandma Gingersnap and Topper both gave him a skeptical look. "Are you joking, Kris?" she asked. "Because Tink could get into trouble alone in a padded room. I thought you knew better than to tease about something like this."

He tried to "ho-ho-ho" his way out of it, but his Santa magic didn't work on my grandmother. "Sorry," he said. "I was being hopeful."

Grandma put her hand on Jax's sleeve. "Thank you again for taking care of her. I know it wasn't easy."

"You're welcome," he said. "But we took care of each other. We're a team."

We smiled while Grandma Gingersnap, my uncle, and Topper eyed us curiously. "Interesting," she said. "Let's get you to the hospital, Tink. And after you recover from your surgery, I'm taking you to a spa."

"No." Jax and I said the word together. We must have said it pretty loudly, too, because other people at the airport turned to look at us. Or that could have been because we were there with Santa. My uncle always got a lot of attention, no matter where he went. He smiled and waved at the onlookers. They smiled back. The man was like catnip for elves of all cultures.

"No," I said, more softly this time. "No more spas. No more facials. No more funky desserts. I want to go to bed, eat Christmas cookies, and rest for a month. Maybe two."

"That sounds like a plan," said Grandma Gingersnap. "And I'm making you soup, along with the cookies. And cocoa. But first, we need to take care of that ankle."

She grabbed the handles of my wheelchair and began pushing me toward the door in heels. After nearly running into several people and a mirrored wall, Topper took over. I let out a sigh of relief.

"Thanks," I said.

"You got it, kiddo. Now let's get you patched up."

THE SURGERY TO repair my ankle sucked. I had a bar and screws inserted to hold my bones together, and I would end up with a huge scar. The only good thing that happened was that Noelle volunteered to be my nurse. She'd forgiven me for what had happened to Bing, and we both cried. We cried about my ankle, too. That may have seemed silly, but my legs had always been one of my best features, and how I'd be scarred and gross. Also, I was riding on a post-nearly-dying rollercoaster of emotions.

"I'm going to look like franken-elf," I said with a sniff. "I'll have a huge scar. It's going to be so ugly."

"At least you aren't green anymore," said Noelle, wiping away a tear. "And even if it looks bad at first, it'll be hardly noticeable later."

"If you say so."

"I do."

"It's silly to be crying over something like this," I said, but I kept crying.

"It's not the scar, Tink. It's the scar on top of everything else."

"You're right. You're so smart. Thanks for not hating me."

She grabbed my hand and squeezed it. "I could never hate you. You're my oldest and dearest friend. I missed you something awful, Tink. I'm glad you're home."

I blinked away a fresh flood of tears. "I missed you, too."

"And look at all the flowers you've received," she said, indicating beautiful bouquets. "Who is this one from?"

It was a gorgeous bouquet of tropical blossoms that smelled as good as it looked. "I have no idea."

She read the card with a frown. "To Mistle Ho from a friend."

Noelle glanced up at me, confused, as she handed me the card. I took it with a smile. "It's a long story."

"It's always a long story." She folded her arms over her chest, getting annoyed on my behalf. "And I can't believe Angelica Frost almost killed you."

"I know, right? Our high school reunions will be super interesting from now on."

She laughed. "It's a little warm in here. Do you want your window open?"

"Yes, please." It was a beautiful November day on the North Pole, but the dome kept it reasonably warm, and the hospital air was stuffy. The window was large and faced downtown. Noelle pulled it open, allowing the cool air to come inside.

"There's no screen," she said. "They take them off when they clean the windows. This one must have been broken or needed replacing. Are you okay with it wide open like this?"

"Yes. It feels great."

"You won't fall out the window, will you? Because you're on the twelfth floor."

I laughed. "Noelle, I'm clumsy, but I'm not that clumsy. Also, thanks to my leg, I can't even walk to the window, let alone fall out of it."

"If you say so." A tap sounded at the door. "That must be Nat. He texted me to let me know he'd be stopping by."

She opened the door and let my former partner, Officer Nat Bing, into the room. He carried two bouquets. He handed one to Noelle, kissed her, and handed the other bouquet to me.

"Hi, Tink," he said.

"Hey, Bing."

Noelle glanced at her watch. "I have to finish my rounds. I'll be back. Buzz me if you need anything."

I gave her a thumbs up. "Will do."

After she left, there was an awkward silence. I took a deep breath, trying to figure out what to say. I went with the most straightforward approach.

"I'm so sorry."

He gave me a crooked smile. "I know. It's fine. I felt like an idiot, but it's all good now. I'm back at work. I have a new partner, Jangle Pine. He's nowhere near as interesting as you."

"Is anyone?"

He laughed. "You set the bar pretty high. Jangle and I are working on an illegal arms-smuggling case. It's fascinating. You wouldn't believe some of the weapons we've confiscated."

I sat up straighter, enjoying his enthusiasm. "Tell me about it. I love hearing about this kind of stuff."

"Well, a lot of it was designed for special ops. Some high-tech crossbows. A spear gun—for use underwater, of all things. A laser gun. A gun hidden in a camera."

"Say 'cheese' and die, right?"

"Exactly," he said. "And a lot of other things, too. Dart guns. Machine guns. Big guns. Small guns. I even saw a pen that can be used as a gun."

"Mightier than the sword?"

"Yep. It's crazy."

The artificial sunlight created by the dome over the North Pole streamed in through my window. It was different than the sunshine in Belize, but I liked it. It felt like home.

"I'm glad things are going well for you," I said.

"Thanks." He snuck a glance over his shoulder and lowered his voice. "And I have some other news. I'm planning to pop the question to Noelle on Christmas. I wanted you to be the first to know. Will you help me set it up?"

"Of course I will," I said. "I'm so happy for you."

A short, sharp stab of sadness hit me unexpectedly. Yes, I was delighted for Bing and my best friend, but Noelle getting married meant everything would change. I didn't quite feel ready for it. I decided to change the subject. I was still on painkillers. I tended to cry a lot when drugged.

"So... what else has been going on at work?"

"They assigned new detectives to the case involving Scarlet's murder. They've made zero progress, as far as I can tell. You and Jax did more while on vacation, which is kind of funny and yet not funny at all."

"We got lucky," I said.

He gave me a skeptical look. "Is that seriously what you think? Tink, you are an amazing detective. You're brave, smart, intuitive, and you take chances when others won't."

"And that's how I ended up like this," I said, pointing to my cast.

"And that's how you ended up breaking up the largest drug-producing operation in the elven world. They shut Petunia and Angelica down completely. They're both in jail."

"That's good news."

"It's excellent news. Do you know how many lives, both elven and human, you may have saved? They were manipulating the veil. They planned to start sending their stuff into the human world. It would have been a nightmare." He shook his head in disbelief. "Oh, and Angelica confessed to poisoning your honeymoon cake. She said she wanted to make you sick, so you'd go home."

"Did she admit to ransacking our room and inviting a bunch of monkeys in for an orgy?"

Bing's eyes widened in surprise. "What? Are you kidding?" When I shook my head, he laughed. "No, she didn't admit to that."

I frowned. "Then who was in our room?"

He shrugged. "I have no idea, but I can't believe how you figured out the clues in this case. The details you notice are amazing. For example, you said in your report that there was a misspelling on the produce boxes."

"Fragilee," I said with a snort. "That was something silly."

He leaned closer, the expression on his handsome face intense. "No, it was important. The boxes marked that way all contained rock candy. The ones spelled correctly did not."

I wrinkled my nose at him. "Are you serious?"

"Yep. It made things a lot easier for the customs guys. They are singing your praises, Tink."

"Well, I'm glad we stopped them," I said. "But it doesn't change the fact that Scarlet died because of me. And you could have died, too, Bing. It's one thing to put myself in danger. It's another to do that to you."

He gave me a playful smack on the arm. "Help me set up this proposal. After that, we're even."

"Speaking of putting yourself in danger..." I deadpanned.

He grinned. "A risk I'm willing to take.

AFTER BING LEFT, a slow parade of visitors came in and out of my room. Jax had meetings all morning to debrief Director O'Reilly, Chief Sleigh, and several big potatoes from Elven High Council. They'd come to the North Pole for the meeting. My uncle attended as well. When Topper showed up after lunch, I figured the meeting was over.

"How did it go?" I asked.

"As well as could be expected." He handed me a peppermint mocha with extra whipped cream and sprinkles on top. I took it with greedy hands.

"Oh, jingle my bells. This is the best thing ever. Have you had hospital coffee? I don't think it's even coffee. It's black, skunky water. Thank you, Topper."

"You're welcome, kiddo," he said, sitting on the chair next to my bed.

I took a long sip of the peppermint mocha and sighed. "I can feel my brain waking up. Tell me about the meeting."

Topper folded his hands over his flat stomach. Even though he was the same age as my uncle, he didn't have Uncle Kris's portly frame. Topper was all muscle. He also had great instincts, which was why he was Uncle Kris's head of security. Topper knew his stuff.

"Well, thanks to you and Jax, we've stopped one of the biggest drug operations in elven history," he said. "But the work isn't done yet. It's like playing whack-a-mole. As soon as you slam one, another pops up to take its place. I hear rumbles that something is going on with the water elves. It seems likely. They can distribute almost everywhere."

"True. Even here and the South Pole, they can go under the ice, right?"

"Exactly. When something is that profitable, someone always seems to be slipping in to fill the void."

"Any news on Scarlet's murder?"

He shook his head. "We got the flash drive when we raided Petunia's compound, but it was corrupted. We don't need it to put Petunia, Angelica, and their gang away, though. We have so much evidence against them that they will spend the rest of their lives behind bars." He paused. "We did find something interesting, though. Guess who Petunia's accountant was?"

"Red?"

He seemed surprised. "You already knew? Yes, he's Scarlet's brother. Red. And he's pretty pissed off about losing his sister and his niece. He's planning to testify about a bunch of mobsters, including a friend of yours."

My eyes widened. "Ganja? But he's been on the straight and narrow for years."

"Five years," said Topper. "I checked. The statute of limitations is seven years. He should be fine if he can lay low for another few years and keep his nose clean."

Ganja must have known. He said he had to make himself scarce for a while.

"What if he has information about Scarlet's murder? I think he knows who may have done it. They were targeting him, not Scarlet."

"I heard about that, and I wish we could offer him a deal, but Ganja is no dummy. He disappeared after Red came to speak with us. I have a feeling we won't hear from him again until that statute of limitations is up."

I frowned. "Then it's up to us to figure it out."

Topper studied me. "You mean it's up to the detectives assigned to the case?"

"Yeah. That's what I meant." I bit my lip. I felt like I was missing something important. Something beyond my grasp. "I keep going back to motive, means, and opportunity. The motive had to do with Ganja, but I'm unclear on what.

The opportunity presented itself at the club. I'm stuck on the means. Have they figured out what killed Scarlet yet?"

He shook his head. "I'm still going with the projectile theory."

"But what kind of projectile disappears?"

He shrugged. "There are quite a few things, but one, in particular, comes to mine. I'll give you a riddle. You remember how much you used to love riddles as a kid?" He cleared his throat. "I'm the daughter of the water, but when I return to the water, I die. Who am I?"

I sent him a dirty look. "Seriously?" He grinned at me. I let out a huff and considered his words. When I got the answer, I sat up so quickly that I nearly fell out of bed. "Ice. She was killed with ice?"

"That's my theory," said Topper.

"It makes sense. But are there guns that shoot ice?"

"There are if you're in special operations. I've seen one called the Polar Piercer. It's a South Pole invention—a specialized sort of dart gun. But instead of darts, it shoots icicles. The icicles are sharp enough to pierce the skin and come in different sizes. The smallest is like a needle."

A needle made of ice. A needle that would melt into a puddle of water—just like the one I'd found beneath Scarlet's head at the club.

I lifted my hands in the air. "That's it! I need to call Jax."

"He's still with Director O'Reilly and Chief Sleigh. You two created a whole pile of paperwork on your little trip. It's going to take hours to sort that out."

"Poor Jax. Better him than me. I'll text him." I sent him the text and furrowed my brow. "But this still doesn't help me figure out who the killer is."

"What have I always told you, Tink? Solving a crime is

like solving a puzzle. Part of it is eliminating what doesn't work, but the other part is about looking at it from all possible angles. Everyone is a suspect. Doubt everyone and don't trust anyone."

"Ganja said something similar to me. I wish I could talk to him."

"You don't need to talk to him. Use that brain of yours. The answer is right in front of you, like the ice dart. I mean, it melted, but it was in front of you."

"I guess."

"When you eliminate those who didn't do it, the person left is the one who did it."

"You make it sound simple, but there are so many possibilities. Where do I start?"

"That part is simple," he said. "Start with the obvious. Who most wanted Ganja dead, and why?"

TWENTY-SIX

After Topper left, the physical therapist, an abnormally perky young elf named Pointy Parker, stopped by to teach me how to use crutches.

"You're young and strong," she said, her dark ponytail swinging back and forth as she measured me. "You'll be fine. Let me grab the crutches, and we'll get started."

I was not fine. After several attempts that resulted in me falling, once on top of Pointy and once onto the lap of an elderly gentleman who seemed rather entertained by the whole thing, Pointy seemed less perky. And all I had on was a holiday-themed hospital gown, my panties exposed to the world. Maybe that's why the old guy found it so amusing.

"Are you okay waiting here for a minute?" asked Pointy, a fine sheen of perspiration on her brow as she helped me into a chair in the hallway. "I want to try a different size. Or maybe a walker. Or maybe a forklift. I don't know."

"I'm fine. I'm not moving," I said. I was perspiring, too, but instead of glistening like Pointy, I sweated like a racehorse. I fanned myself with my hand, and Pointy high-tailed it down the hall. I wondered if she would return and wished I'd brought my cell phone with me, and that was when someone came out of the elevator. An unexpected visitor. Director O'Reilly.

"Hello, Tink," he said, walking toward me. He wore a long coat, a bowler hat, and a scarf. He wasn't used to the cold at the North Pole, and air elves had a funny way of walking on their tiptoes when they weren't hovering. They looked like ballet dancers but chubbier and with shorter legs.

I waved at him. "Hey, there. What a nice surprise."

"I wanted to check on you," he said, perching delicately in the chair next to me. He sat on the edge of his seat, his body turned toward me. He looked uncomfortable. I wondered if it hurt air elves to lean back on their wings. Maybe it did.

"Thanks," I said. "I'm fine. How did the meeting go?"

"As well as could be expected. You did fine work, Ms. Holly. Unfortunately, Ganja Green, one of our main targets, has disappeared. We had everything set up to catch him in Atlantic City next week, but our plan won't work now. He's gone, and you can hardly go undercover as a stripper on crutches, now, can you?"

"Ha. I can barely walk on crutches. I think my physical therapist may have run away."

He smiled, but it didn't quite meet his eyes. "Where is he, Tink?"

"Who?" I asked, genuinely confused.

"Ganja Green."

Something felt off here. "I don't know. The last time I saw him was at the airport in Belize."

"Trust me." Like a butterfly trapped in a net, I heard a weird fluttering sound. The sound came from Director

O'Reilly. His coat covered his wings, and they moved uselessly inside.

"I do trust you, sir. And you should trust me."

His lips twisted into the barest hint of a smile. "Of course I do. Thank you, Ms. Holly, for all your hard work. I've spoken with my team at the EBI. You're on track to be a full-fledged agent soon. As soon as you can start training, the job is yours."

"Wow. Thanks," I said as he got to his feet.

"You're welcome, Ms. Holly. I'll be in touch. And I expect you to be in touch, too, especially if you hear from Ganja. You know where your loyalties lie, right?"

"I do."

As I watched him walk back to the elevator, a sickening realization hit me. Director O'Reilly had on a coat that covered his wings. That's why I'd heard the sound like a trapped butterfly when he'd sat next to me. But seeing him in that coat made everything come together in my mind.

The wings under his coat made it look like Director O'Reilly was misshapen. Like he had a hump. And the hump was right in the middle of his back—exactly like whoever pretended to be Gus Gravy the night Scarlet was murdered.

"Jiminy Christmas," I said to myself.

Director O'Reilly pressed the button for the elevator. When he turned back to look at me, I tried to keep my expression neutral. "Bye," I said, giving him a little wave.

He nodded in return, but I saw something cold and evil in his beady eyes. It terrified me. Director O'Reilly was not the friendliest guy in the world, but why would he kill Gus? And why did he try to kill Ganja?

As soon as he got onto the elevator, I grabbed my

crutches and attempted to speed back to my room. I needed my phone. I had to call Jax.

It was not easy. I swayed back and forth, ran into two walls, and nearly fell several times, but finally, I made it to my room. I dove into the bed, my crutches clattering to the floor. Laying on my stomach, I grabbed my phone and called Jax. I'd just pressed his name on speed dial when I heard the door of my room close behind me. Hands shaking, I discreetly shoved my phone under my pillow, hoping Jax picked up. I felt I knew who'd followed me into my room, and when I turned around, I realized I was right.

Director O'Reilly stood there, almost pulsating with fury. He took off his hat and set it on a chair.

"How did you figure it out?" he asked, taking off his coat and letting out a tiny sound of pleasure as his wings fluttered and he was lifted into the air. It probably felt the way I did when taking my bra off after a long day. "What was the clue?"

I saw no point in pretending. I pointed to his back. "Your wings. Gus Gravy had a lump. He was supposed to be Quasimodo, but the lump was in the wrong place. Today, with that coat on, you had the same lump."

"I see," he said, unraveling the scarf from his thin neck. "Our wings are both a blessing and a curse. We can fly, but not too high. We can't soar, and yet we're not earthbound either. And that's what killed my son. Well, that and Ganja Green."

My eyes widened. "Your son was the elf who tried to fly off the roof of his casino?"

Tears filled his eyes, and his lips wobbled under his mustache. "Flippy was there to celebrate his 21st birthday. He had no experience with alcohol. He thought he could fly."

"How is that Ganja's fault?"

His face reddened in fury. "It was a rooftop bar, but there was an incident in the casino that night. There was no security there. If they'd been in place, they could have stopped him. His friends could have stopped him. And after Flippy died, it destroyed my wife. My soulmate. She killed herself. And, according to our so-called justice system, no one was to blame."

"That's horrible. And you took matters into your own hands?"

He nodded. "Yes. I tried to punish them through legal means. The system failed me. So I took care of the friends first. A sleigh accident for Seamus. A freak allergic reaction for Paulette. A drug overdose for Ruby."

I clapped a hand over my mouth in shock. "You killed both Ruby and Scarlet? As well as Gus and those other innocent people?"

"Gus and Scarlet were the only innocents. The others deserved to die."

"You're sick. You need help."

"No, I need to kill Ganja. I need to make him pay. But I have some loose ends to tie up. Namely, a spoiled little Christmas elf who doesn't know when to start minding her own business."

He fluttered over to me, his scarf in his tiny hands. I edged back as far as I could on the bed. I'd never felt so helpless. I couldn't run. I couldn't hide. I reached for the buzzer for the nurses' station, but before I could press it, Director O'Reilly wrapped his scarf around my neck. I thrashed, fighting against him, but he was surprisingly strong. I remembered Topper telling me he'd been special ops, which was why he'd known how to use the Polar Piercer dart gun.

And I remembered something else.

Once, my old boss, Puck McHappy, had gotten into a bar fight with an air elf. "He bit me," said Puck, showing me his scars. "I nearly lost a finger. I didn't know what to do, but now I do."

"What?" I'd asked, slightly drunk at the time.

"I'd bite him back," he'd said with a grin. "Air elves aren't expecting it. They're sneaky little pests but have a low pain tolerance."

As Director O'Reilly tightened the noose around my neck, causing me to see stars, I did what Puck had recommended. I bit down on Director O'Reilly's finger—hard. I mean, I chomped down.

I felt his skin give way almost immediately and tasted his blood. Director O'Reilly screamed, letting go of the scarf as he tried to pull his finger out of my mouth. I kept biting down.

I'm not sure exactly what happened next. I must have exceptionally strong teeth, or air elves have exceedingly dainty bones. Either way, I heard a crack, and suddenly half of Director O'Reilly's finger came off in my mouth. He howled in agony, buzzing around the room and bouncing off the walls. I spit out the finger, took the scarf off my neck, and rang for the nurses.

Director O'Reilly continued to fly around the room, blind with panic and pain. I realized air elves are even worse than Christmas elves in an emergency. And something unexpected happened.

Director O'Reilly flew headfirst, straight out the open window of my room.

"Oh, snap," I said, struggling to get to my feet. I found one crutch, but it was enough for me to hobble to the window. I peeked out, and what I saw would live on in my nightmares for years to come. Director O'Reilly had hit the flagpole in front of North Pole General on his way down. It had impaled him directly through his torso. The worst part? He was still alive. He grasped the pole as if trying to extricate himself, but he looked like a moth pinned to a board in some macabre collection of specimens. His eyes met mine, and although I was high above him, I watched him die. His gaze became vacant, and his hands stopped their futile attempts. They fell gently to his sides, and his head tilted back. And that's when the worst thing of all happened.

He smiled. The pain was over at last.

TWENTY-SEVEN

I'm not sure how long I stood there staring at Director O'Reilly's body. A crowd of elves had formed below, and someone was pounding on the door to my room. Director O'Reilly must have locked it when he came inside.

I turned, planning to hop over and open it. Before I could make it there, it flew open, and Jax rushed in, phone in hand. His gaze darted frantically around the room, and when it landed on me, I thought his knees might give out.

"Tink."

I must have looked a sight, with blood all over my face. I probably had bruises on my neck as well. I started to shake. I knew from experience that this was a post-adrenaline rush. Also, I may have been going into shock.

"What happened?" he asked. When he realized I could no longer stand, he used his one good arm to help me to the bed. "Is that your blood?"

I shook my head. At some point, I'd started bawling. I waved my hand toward the window. Jax looked outside, and then turned back to me.

"Jiminy Christmas," he said.

"Ditto." I croaked the words. "He tried to kill me."

"What did you do?" he asked. "O'Reilly was special ops. A trained killer."

I shrugged, picking up the remains of Director O'Reilly's finger and showing it to Jax. "I bit back."

Jax lowered himself next to me on the bed, his face so pale I thought he might pass out. "You bit off his finger."

"Desperate times," I said. "And it's what Puck McHappy said to do if I ever got in a fight with an air elf."

"I owe Puck a drink."

"I owe Puck my life."

HOSPITAL SECURITY ARRIVED, and so did my grandmother, my uncle, and Topper. Jax was meeting with Chief Sleigh and the Elven High Council members at the North Pole to explain what had happened.

Someone must have given my grandmother a sedative. She was handling this way too well. "He deserved to have more than his finger bitten off," she said. "That horrible, horrible elf."

"Well, he was also impaled by a flagpole and didn't die on impact, so there's that, too," I said.

She shrugged. "I guess. I'm glad you didn't die. Again." She looked up at a painting of daisies on the wall. "Are those flowers talking? I think they're talking."

I looked at my uncle in alarm. "Oops," he said. "We must have double-dosed her. We'd better take your grandmother home. I'm proud of you, Tink. Then again, I'm always proud of you."

He kissed my cheek. Grandma Gingersnap kissed me, too. "You're getting discharged tomorrow. I'm wrapping you in bubble wrap, and you're not leaving my house. Mr. Rhett Butler and I will take such good care of you. Did I tell you I love my kitty cat? That was the most thoughtful gift ever, darling."

After kissing me several more times, my uncle hustled her out the door. Topper and I watched them go. Topper had his hands in his pockets, his expression downcast.

"I'm sorry about your friend," I said. "I know you and Director O'Reilly were buddies when you served in special ops."

"Yeah, we went way back. He changed after Flippy died, and his wife killed herself. He wasn't the same person anymore. I thought he was depressed. I didn't realize he was murderous." He sighed. "You were clever to keep your phone on. Jax heard everything. We could have used the evidence at trial if you hadn't pushed O'Reilly out the window."

"I did not push him. I bit off his finger."

"I know," he said with a laugh. "I was messing with you. You did good work, Tink. And now we can tell all those people whose family members he killed that he was the one responsible—starting with Flo Dazzle. I'm figuring you'd want to be the one to tell her."

"I would," I said.

"That's what a thought. He killed her daughter and her granddaughter. And Red has become a great informant. It's all ending well. I mean, except for all the deaths and the Director of the EBI falling out a window. It does feel like poetic justice, though."

Justice.

I remembered Ganja using that word. But was it justice? Flo would never have her daughter or granddaughter back, but maybe Red could turn his life around.

I'd just started dozing later that evening when Jax showed up. A security guard was posted outside my door in case anyone else tried to kill me today. Jax's broad shoulders sagged with exhaustion. I shifted over so he could join me and patted the spot next to me on my bed. He had a cast on his arm and a sling, but I'd never seen him look so sad.

"What's wrong?" I asked.

"They want me to take over O'Reilly's job."

I blinked at him in surprise. "Are you serious? That's good, right?"

"I don't know." He sighed. "It complicates things. You're on track to be an agent, and I know it's what you want. I would still be your boss."

"Oh. I see." I pondered the implications. "Well, my grandmother wants me to choose a different profession. She'd be delighted if I quit."

He kissed the top of my head, and I snuggled closer to him. "You need to be an agent. You were made for the job. You're incredible. And I need to take this job, at least temporarily. The Bureau is a mess. If I don't help, I'm not sure who will. But I'm not certain where it would leave us."

"It is a conundrum."

"And there is the matter of my family, too," he said. "According to my mother, my father was warming up to the diplomatic position. He's going to hate this."

I put my hand on his chest. "You need to do what you think is best for you."

"I want to do what's best for us."

"What's best for you is best for us."

He stared at me for a long moment before swallowing hard. "Can you reach inside my pocket?"

I fluttered my eyelashes at him. "Uh, Jax, I've heard that line before…"

He rolled his eyes. "Just do it, Tink. I only have one working arm, and you're lying on it. Reach in my jacket pocket, please." I did as instructed and pulled out a small box. Inside was his mother's rochtar diamond.

"What's this?"

"I want you to have it."

"But Jax—"

"As a promise. For later. Can you give me some time? I'll figure this out. I swear."

I put the ring on my finger. "I can give you some time. I'll give you all the time you need."

He leaned closer and kissed me. And it was everything. It made me feel more befuddled than the powerful painkillers my doctor had ordered for me.

"We'll find a way to work this out," he said. "FML, Tink."

I grinned up at him, the diamond sparkling on my finger and a sense of contentment flowing over me that had nothing at all to do with the narcotics.

"FML, Jax. FML."

For the first book in The Tink Holly Chronicles, REBEL WITHOUT A CLAUS, scan here:

ABOUT THE AUTHOR

Abigail Drake is the award-winning author of seventeen novels, but she didn't start her career in writing. She majored in Japanese and economics in college, and spent years traveling the world, collecting stories wherever she visited. She collected a husband from Istanbul on her travels, too, and he happens to be her favorite souvenir.

Abigail is a coffee addict, a puppy wrangler, and the mother of three adult sons. To learn more about Abigail, please visit her website: http://www.abigaildrake.net

The Tink Holly Chronicles

Claus And Effect

Rebel Without a Claus

Sultans From Space

Betting on an Alien Prince

Gift of an Alien Prince

The South Side Stories

The Dragonsong Law Offices

The Hocus Pocus Magic Shop

The Enchanted Garden Cafe

Passports and Promises

Delayed Departure

Flying Solo

New Heights

Saying Goodbye

The Passports and Promises Series Boxed Set

A Dog Names Al Capone

Hearts, Flowers, and a Dog Named Al Capone

Love, Chocolate, and a Dog Named Al Capone

Lola Flannigan

Traveller

Young Adult Fiction

The Bodyguard

Starr Valentine

Tiger Lily

Non-Fiction

The Reformed Pantser's Guide to Plotting

For more about Abigail, visit her website:

https://abigaildrake.net